JUST FOR A LITTLE WHILE

FIONA COLE

Copyright © 2021 by Fiona Cole

All rights reserved.

Interior Design: Indie Girl Promotions

Editing: Kelly Allenby, Readers Together

No part of this book may be reproduced or transmitted in any form or by any means, electronic or mechanical, including photocopying, recording, or by any information storage and retrieval system without written permission of the author, except for the use of brief quotations in a book review.

This is a work of fiction. Names, characters, businesses, places, events and incidents are either the products of the author's imagination or used in a fictitious manner. Any resemblance to actual persons, living or dead, actual events, or locales is entirely coincidental.

To Willow.

You're an amazing woman and one of the best parts of this community. Thank you for always being willing to help.

ONE

Arabella

"You're moving in with your uncle next week."

"What uncle?"

"Seriously, Arabella?" My mother looked at me like I'd grown a second head.

"Seriously, Diana," I snarked back. Something about traveling Europe by yourself made answering to parents a million times harder. "You have a sister who is a lesbian, and Dad is an only child."

"Uncle Willem," Dad said before Mom could snap back.

"Willem isn't my uncle."

"Close enough."

"A stepbrother from one of Grandpa's many marriages from fifteen years ago, hardly counts. Were you even in the same house for long? Is he even old enough to watch me?"

"For the love of God, Arabella," my mom muttered.

"He's thirty-three. So, old enough."

"When do you even talk to him? In between surgeries while you live at the hospital?"

"Please stop arguing, Arabella," my dad said, rubbing his eyes. "He's the closest thing you have to an uncle, and since Grandpa died, family is sparse. So, take what you can get."

1

"Don't I get a say in it?" I argued.

Why bother asking my opinion when they didn't want to hear it anyway. They never had before when making a decision for me.

"What will you say, Arabella?" Mom asked. "You've been back from your backpacking adventures for two weeks and start school in less than a month. You sold your car to traipse around Europe for six months. Uncle Willem lives right off campus and can give you a ride if need be."

"You could always help me with another one. Pay for half like you did the first, and I'd pay you back."

Both parents knew better and silently shook their heads, moving on without even entertaining the idea.

"He was nice enough to offer when we told him you somehow *forgot* to apply for student housing," Dad said.

I shrugged completely unrepentant. "Whoops."

What can I say? I kind of hoped they wouldn't hold me to my word of going to college, and maybe if I didn't have a place to stay, then I wouldn't have to go.

My world history class my junior year had sparked a light in me I didn't know existed. From then on, all I could think about was traveling the world any way possible. I delayed my first year of college after high school and worked two jobs to save money. My parents let me know they wouldn't be helping in any way if I put off college.

It would have been perfect, except my best friend, Felicity, got sick before we left, and the trip that we'd planned on splitting, had turned into a solo purchase. One I couldn't afford.

"You're not getting out of this. A deal is a deal," Mom reminded me.

They'd ended up giving me the small amount I couldn't make up in such short notice to cover Felicity's portion, but I had to apply to college and be back in time to start the fall semester. They'd made me apply before I left, and I would have promised almost anything to get out that door.

"I know," I grumbled.

"We thought you could leave a few weeks early and look for a job. Willem said you didn't have to pay any rent, but you will be responsible for taking care of yourself."

"Will I have a curfew? Or will I be allowed some freedom?"

"Jesus." Mom's arms flew in the air before pacing away.

I was being snotty, and I knew it. I just hated this pressure of a life I didn't choose closing in on me. Especially after months of answering to no one but myself.

None of it was new. They wanted me to be a certain way and *encouraged*, as Mom put it, me to be better. I thought I was fine the way I was.

In the very stereotypical fashion, I tended to push back to keep them at a distance so their disappointment stung less.

"Will you be taking me? Or am I flying? If I'm flying, how will I know it's him when I see him. It's been so long. A stranger could come claim me, and I'd never know."

My dad merely stared, used to my antics. "It's been two years, I hardly think you could forget how he looks," he deadpanned. "And you'll be flying."

I definitely didn't forget how he looked.

I'd only seen him a handful of times at holidays when he could make it out to Denver, but the last time I'd seen him, I'd been old enough to understand attraction. It wasn't like I was putting my non-existent daddy issues on him by finding him attractive. It was more factual—objective. Uncle Willem was hot.

He'd been tall, broad, dark hair, and ocean eyes. His square jaw had been clean-shaven with his hair slicked back. It'd been thanksgiving, and while I'd lounged around in my leggings and giant sweater, he'd looked put together in slacks and a button up.

Too bad I'd been into guys just as savage as my personality. So, while my feminine body recognized his looks, I'd been able to brush it aside.

I hadn't talked to him the whole time, fully entrenched in my peak teen years of attitude. We'd had one moment when we crossed paths in the kitchen.

"*Nice nose ring,*" he'd said.

I'd given him my signature smirk and walked away.

"What about Todd and my friends."

"Todd?" Dad asked.

"My boyfriend."

"Please," Mom scoffed. "If you expect me to think you'd want to stay for *Todd*, you must think I'm dumber than rocks."

"You have a boyfriend?" Dad asked. "Since when? Have we met him?"

"Since before I left. He came to my graduation party."

My dad's face screwed up when he remembered the polar opposite of me. "The football player?"

"If Todd can be your *boyfriend,*" Mom added air quotes for good measure, "while you're overseas for six months, then he can handle you going to college."

"Listen, Arabella," my dad said, ready to bargain to make it end. "You put in an honest effort at school, earn half the money for a decent car and we'll pay the rest and make sure you have an apartment by summer.

At this point it was all a waste of time to argue. Even my own stubbornness had its limits. And the apartment didn't matter—it was the promise of freedom and independence.

"Fine. I'll pack this week, but I'm heading out to enjoy my last Saturday with friends."

"Be back by midnight," my mom called to my retreating back. "And we still need to talk about the tattoo I saw in one of your pictures. As well as the topless beach."

"*Topless what?*" my dad screeched.

I chuckled but kept walking to grab my things.

All-in-all, maybe leaving home earlier than expected would be good. After having a taste of freedom, every rule that used to be my norm felt like a shackle tying me in place.

So, I'd move to Cincinnati with *Uncle* Willem and utilize the roof over my head. He could stay home and sip his tea by the fire while he read a good novel on how to tie the best Windsor knot. I'd be out and about and working my ass off to afford a place of my own.

I just needed to keep my eye on the prize and hope good ole Uncle Willem didn't try to control me like some misplaced father figure.

As far as I knew, he was single with no kids. So, it'd be just him and me. I planned on not being there as much as possible.

TWO

Willem

"I can't tonight, Tessa. My niece is coming in."

"Niece? Since when do you have a niece? And how have you not told me about any family? We've been together for almost a month?"

By together, she meant fucking. We'd been fucking for a few weeks—on occasion. It was time to cut ties, and maybe having Arabella here would be the perfect excuse. I should have done it sooner, like the first night I realized how incompatible we were. I'd tested her limits and lightly fisted her hair, and she'd winced with a whine that damn near stole my erection. It wasn't like I wanted to tie her up and cane her, but I was a big guy with a big appetite, and I liked a woman who could handle both sides of me—the one that tortured with soft touches and teasing kisses and the one that gripped so hard I left bruises as I fucked you into next week. I liked a woman who wouldn't cave to me throughout the day, only to kneel and beg me for release later that night.

"She's my stepbrother's kid. A stepbrother from my mom's last marriage. Not technically my niece," I found myself explaining anyway.

"Well," she huffed. "If you ever need to escape the brat, just come on over here. I'll help you relax."

She said it like Arabella was a ten-year-old girl with pigtails in need of a babysitter. I almost snorted at the thought but shoved it down.

"Yeah. I'll let you know."

I quickly got off the phone and rubbed a hand down my face, my mind wandering back to Arabella. Part of me wanted to laugh at Tessa's accurate description of Arabella. Harry said her trip to Europe helped Arabella grow up. Sort of.

But that wasn't the biggest problem. No. The bigger problem was that Arabella looked nothing like a little bratty girl. I'd pulled up her Instagram and, after realizing I'd been scrolling for ten minutes, I'd shut it down faster than a kid being walked in on jerking off.

Only ten minutes, and I'd kind of lost myself a bit. I'd lost myself in admiring how bold she looked—free…sexy.

Long gone was the snotty teen with braces who'd refused to acknowledge I existed at Thanksgiving. Even further from the girl I remembered when I'd visit between trips abroad.

For those ten minutes, nothing else existed except the girl in Instagram worthy pics all over Europe. She rarely smiled and wore her attitude—or brattiness as Harry explained—hooked on the corner of her mouth that tipped up in a smirk in almost every picture.

The doorbell pulled me from that rabbit hole, and I jumped up from the couch, jerking my head side to side to make sure nothing was out of place. I didn't know what I was looking for, but I rarely had company, and for the first time, I looked at my house from the perspective of an almost twenty-year-old.

Not finding anything too damning, I went to open the door.

On the other side, I found the same girl who entranced me with each photo, her eyes—and half her face—covered by a pair of aviator glasses. The reddish tint in her hair caught in the sunlight, making her almost look like a true redhead instead of the lighter brunette I remembered.

Her eyebrows peeked up above the rim of her glasses, and she looked me up and down. I stood taller as if under inspection and, with a lot more subtlety than her, did the same.

Her high-top chucks were only laced up halfway, leaving the top to flare out over her thin ankles. All her hiking pictures weren't just for show. I could see her defined legs encased in tight black leggings, and it made me wonder how her thighs would flex around a man's waist. As if that wasn't bad enough, the top of her leggings stopped just below her belly button, leaving a slim line of her stomach exposed under a plain, white, crop top T-shirt. It was like she found a baggy, little boy's undershirt. However, it wasn't baggy enough to hide the fact that she wasn't wearing a bra, her pert nipples poking against the fabric.

I almost got caught up on the sight, but quickly jerked my gaze away with a sharp reprimand.

Niece. Niece. Niece.

Not really your niece.

Fine. Harry's daughter.

A man you respect. His daughter.

Thankfully, she was still taking her time looking me over, completely unrepentant.

I almost laughed.

"You look different."

My head tipped, thrown by those being the first words she said. "Umm...hi. And thank you. I think?" I stepped aside and grabbed one of the bags sitting next to her on the pavement.

That smirk I saw in so many pics made an appearance as she rolled her suitcase through the door.

"Wait. What does that mean?" I asked, closing the door.

She turned and shoved her glasses to the top of her head, exposing light brown eyes, thankfully not like Harry's, and shrugged. "Last time I saw you, you were all buttoned up and clean-shaven."

Just for a Little While

Rubbing my hand across the thick scruff covering my jaw, I couldn't help but still wonder if she was insulting me. I grew my beard out over the summer and kept going back and forth over shaving before school. I opened my mouth to ask her opinion but quickly shoved the question down. "I always try to look my best when I see your dad."

I wasn't very close with Harry, but he was the closest I had to family—the only family I had left. We were very different, but it hadn't stopped us from getting along when our parents were married. He'd been the normal and relaxed in a chaotic time and had been nice enough to include an eleven-year-old boy while he was a senior in high school.

I respected him and the life he created. He had a good wife and a good job. When he'd called letting me know Arabella was coming here for school, I offered up whatever he'd needed. He'd done the same for me once, and it felt good to finally repay him.

"Cool," she answered simply.

Rather than push the subject, I nodded with a tight smile. "I'll show you your room."

I grabbed her rolling suitcase and led her up the flight of stairs, each one creaking under my weight while barely making a noise for her.

"The dresser and closet are empty. The bathroom is the next door over and yours to use however you like. I have one in my bedroom, and the guest one is downstairs."

"Entertain a lot?" she muttered, looking out the floor to ceiling windows.

"No. I don't have many guests. I just wanted to let you know you could leave your stuff out on the counter."

She turned, her lips in a tight smile. "Cool."

I fought to keep from reprimanding her. I remembered being an arrogant shit too. Hell, some still thought I was—specifically, Tessa.

"There's also a pool out back. It rarely gets used, but

someone comes to take care of it. Feel free to use it as you want."

Another tight smile accompanied by a nod.

"So, yeah. Go ahead and get settled, and then we can grab dinner in a couple hours. There's a bar down the street."

"Uhhh, I'm only nineteen," she informed like she thought I was dumb.

I was aware.

"It's more like a pub. Doesn't become a bar until later. You'll be fine."

"Cool."

My irritation at the word bled through, and I stood in the doorway, my brow slowly rising as a reprimand as if waiting for more. She plopped on the bed, almost dragging my attention back to her shirt and the way her small tits bounced from the motion, but I held strong.

Finally, she caved and shrugged, running her hands down her thighs. "Thank you. I'll be ready around six?"

"Six is good," I said, barely holding back my victorious smile. "If you need me, I'll be in my office. It's the third door down. My room is at the end of the hall."

With that, I turned, closing the door behind me, heading back to my office, smile firmly in place.

By the time six rolled around, I made sure I was downstairs in the living room waiting for her. She'd stayed in her room for the most part, although I heard her leave occasionally and rummage in the bathroom.

She'd changed her clothes to black jeans and a tank-top tucked in, thankfully with a bra.

Jesus, I felt like an old pervert.

"Ready?"

"Yup."

"Are you okay with walking?" I asked, looking at her chunky, heeled boots.

"Yeah. I can walk everywhere in these."

Just for a Little While

"You have a car, right?" she asked as I locked the door behind us.

"I do. It's just nice out, and I like to walk when I can. Also, parking can be a bitch in the area with all the students. It's not bad now since it's summer, but come fall, there won't be a free spot."

"Makes sense."

We walked the four blocks in silence, but it didn't seem to bother her. She took in the older homes and shading trees. Every once in a while, a glimpse of campus would peek through the buildings. When we arrived, I asked for a booth toward the back where it was quieter.

She ordered a water and raised a brow when I ordered a beer. I raised one in return, waiting for her to say something. When she didn't, I finally broke the silence.

"So, where's your car? I remember you having one last time I was there."

"I sold it for extra money to travel."

"Makes sense."

A small indent formed between her brows. "You think so?"

"Yeah, of course. I traveled after high school and didn't have shit for money. I'd have sold a car if I had one, too."

She laughed, her lips still somehow in a smirk. I knew she'd had a good life—good experiences, which didn't always make a happy person. But part of me wondered if Arabella didn't smile because her friends expected her to be cool and trendy over not really wanting to. I wasn't that much older than her, but I still remembered the pressures of my peers, and that trend among people her age only increased over the more recent years. It was all about who you portrayed over who you really were.

Her personality screamed 'fuck you,' but it kind of felt like a veneer to keep people at a distance.

"Hell, there are days I still think about selling it, so I can travel more. But then I have my job teaching, so it might not go well."

"What do you teach?"

"A few classes, but global economics is the big one. I also teach some basic economics classes, too."

"Cool."

This time the word didn't grate on my nerves. She perked up and really meant it. She sat taller and brushed her hair back behind her ears, and for the first time, Arabella looked at me.

"What's been your favorite place you've traveled?"

"Oh, boy." I leaned back in the booth and mentally ran through fifteen years of travel, my focus faltering under the full weight of her attention. "Probably London or Scotland."

"All of Scotland or a specific place?"

"I can't pick a favorite place in Scotland. I won't do it." I crossed my arms and turned my nose up like a petulant child, and the earth moved.

Arabella laughed.

Her perfectly shaped pout parted into a perfectly shaped smile. Her head dropped back, and the pale length of her neck moved with the soft, happy sound that fell from her open mouth. It only lasted a moment, but it hit like a physical blow, creating a crack in my own facade, letting the truth trickle in.

I was fucked with this woman in my house.

Because she was a woman. Sitting before me, letting pieces of her true self slip free, she wasn't just a girl. She was a woman, and that knowledge was dangerous.

"I worked at a shipping dock in a few places while I traveled Scotland," she explained. "It was probably the cheapest place we went because of their open camping rules. We set up tents over staying in hotels or hostels."

"I remember the few odd jobs I'd have. I was a bartender for a week in Paris. Didn't know any French, but made it work."

"I was a bartender in London for a month. With all the pubs, it seemed like the best option."

"Do you plan on traveling more?" I asked.

"God, yes. I'd have never come home, but I needed help

with money when my friend had to cancel. My parents said they'd cover what I was short if I agreed to college this year."

"That helps explain the chip on your shoulder since you arrived."

She tried to hide another soft laugh by dropping her head, letting her hair fall around her face. When she looked up, she cringed, her brown eyes peeking through the strands of her hair. "Sorry about that. I guess I can still be a bitch. "

"It's okay. I can be a bitch too," I joked, using a feminine voice.

It did the job, relieving any tension that formed from her talking about why she was there.

"Speaking of jobs. I need one."

"There's no rush. You just got here."

"It's the whole reason I'm here early. So I can get a job to start earning money to replace the car I sold."

"What? Just so you can sell it again next summer?"

She shrugged, not denying it, making me laugh.

She looked side to side as if seeing the place for the first time. The slightly sticky wood floors, dim lights, hodge-podge of patrons, ranging from families with kids, to the stray college student, to old bikers at the bar.

"I'll apply here."

"Are they hiring?"

"Don't know. Let's find out," she said, waggling her brows like my question was issued as a challenge. "Hey," she called to a passing waiter. "You hiring?"

"I don't think so." He looked her up and down with a spark of interest. "But, let me go ask."

And that was how I ended up walking home next to a gloating Arabella, freshly hired after not even having to fill out an application.

Damn, she was impressive.

And impressed by a woman wasn't something I'd experienced in a long time. If ever.

THREE

Arabella

"So, today is day five. How are you holding up?" my best friend, Felicity, asked.

I clutched the phone between my ear and shoulder and tied my Doc Martins. "It's...not horrible. But I haven't done much beyond one day of training for this job."

"How's living with Uncle Willem? Has he set a curfew yet?"

"He's not my uncle." Making the clarification didn't do much to justify how wrong my attraction to him was. Uncle or not, I could list another ten reasons why fantasizing about him was not a good idea. "And it's not bad. We had dinner that first night and honestly, I haven't seen him much. He's at the school or in his office for the most part."

"Nice. Freedom all the way."

"Yeah." I did my best to sound excited, but I didn't know if it was because Felicity was on the phone so far away or what, but loneliness hit me. "He seems cool, though. I wouldn't mind seeing him now and then."

"I mean, girl. I checked out his Instagram. Although a very limited selection, the man is fucking fine. I wouldn't mind having him for dinner either. Good thing he's not my uncle."

"He's not my uncle."

"So you keep saying," she teased.

"Shut up."

"Will you tuck me in, Uncle Willem?" she mocked in a breathy voice.

"Oh, my god. I'd slap you if you were here," I laughed.

"Well, if it makes you feel any better, I wish you were. Todd has a new fuck toy, and she's annoying as hell."

"Ew. Although I'm not surprised."

When I let Todd know I was getting ready to leave again, he let me know he couldn't keep holding out and broke it off. Honestly, I couldn't have cared less. Sometimes, I'd been like my dad and forgot I even had a boyfriend when I hopped around Europe.

"Hope she likes giving blow jobs without receiving," Felicity joked.

"Right?"

"Miss you, bitch," Felicity said quietly.

"I miss you too. Plan to come see me soon?"

"For sure. Maybe Uncle Willem can pick me up from the airport for a quickie."

"Gross." I made gagging noises, making her laugh. "All right, perv. I've got to go to work."

"All right. Look hot. Show the girls."

"What girls?"

"Just because you're not a D cup like me, doesn't mean you don't have anything to shake. Make yo money."

"Will do."

We said our goodbyes, and I headed out the door, wondering if I'd see Willem tonight when I got home. It'd probably be for the best if I didn't.

The bar was a perfect place to work. They're open lunch until late at night, so hours could be flexible when school started. Add in that I could walk, and it was everything I needed. My first day had only been two hours of training with Amber. Any nerves about my first full day eased when I walked in and saw her blonde ponytail swinging.

She got me set up serving a small section, letting me know that if the bar got busy to help out, but only with beer orders. Apparently, under twenty-one-year-olds couldn't sell anything other than beer over the bar.

Halfway through my shift, we hit a lull, and she introduced me to another waitress, Gia, and the bartender, Xander. Gia looked like a replica of Amber, especially when they walked side by side and their white-blonde ponytails swayed in unison. Xander had been the guy who I'd stopped to ask about the job that first day, and he probably made a crap-ton of tips from the ladies, and men, at the bar. Hell, he wasn't even serving me, and I wanted to tip him for providing eye-candy throughout the shift.

More than once, I found myself wondering how old he was and if I could fit both hands around his bicep. Another time or two, when he wandered out from behind the bar, I'd see if I could detect the bulge behind his jeans.

Unfortunately, I also found myself comparing his clean-shaven jaw to Willem's.

I shut that shit down quick but couldn't quite stop it from happening completely.

"So, what brings you to Cincinnati, new girl?" Gia asked.

"College."

"Join the club," they all said in unison.

"Ugh," I groaned my displeasure.

"Not a fan?" Xander asked, laughing.

"Nope. My parents cornered me into it."

"Bummer."

"Are you housing in the dorms?" Amber asked.

"No. I *forgot* to apply in hopes it would stop me from coming. But my un—dad's stepbrother," I corrected before saying uncle, "is a professor at the school, and I'm staying with him."

"Who is it?"

"Willem Deander."

A chorus of squeals and excitement erupted from the duo.

Xander stepped back and winced, covering his ears. "I'm going to head back over there," he said, escaping the high pitch.

"Oh, my god. Seriously? He's so hot," Gia squealed.

"He's the hottie of economics."

"Really?"

"Totally. There's a hot professor in almost every department, but it's totally a tie between Dr. Deander and Dr. Pierce in the science department as the hottest professors of the school."

"Yeah, but Dr. Pierce is married now," Gia whined.

"To one of his students," Amber said, waggling her brows. "It makes me hold on to hope I still have a shot with one of the hotties. Maybe Dr. Deander will come in to see you. We'll meet eyes across the room and fall madly in love," she said dramatically.

"So romantic," Gia added.

"Yeah," I agreed half-heartedly. I imagined the scenario and the embers of a low fire burned in my chest. My fingers twitched to shove her aside and let her know that would never happen. Willem wouldn't be interested in a blonde bimbo.

Jesus.

Taking a deep breath, I calmed the burning jealousy and shut that cattiness down. I may have a snotty attitude, but I was never a bitch. Especially not to other girls just because they liked a guy.

Thankfully, all further fantasies stopped being voiced when a swarm of patrons came in and work picked up again.

The last two hours had me running from one place to another until I was dead on my feet. The walk home felt a lot longer than the walk there.

However, when I walked in, I was met with the nice surprise of Willem sitting on the couch, his feet propped on the coffee table watching the Travel Channel.

"Hey, stranger," he greeted, looking over the back of the couch.

"Hey."

"Long day at work?"

"Yeah, but I'm proud to say, I only messed up twice and flirted my way out of both situations."

He laughed, shaking his head. "There's some pizza on the counter if you're hungry."

As if on cue, my stomach rumbled. "That sounds awesome."

"Grab a beer and come watch about Prague."

"I'm nineteen."

He gave me a look that let me know no one would believe I hadn't drunk before. "I've seen your Instagram and been an eighteen-year-old in Europe. I have no doubt you can handle a beer."

"You looked at my Instagram?"

"Yeah, you're my niece."

"I'm definitely not your niece."

A moment stretched where I leaned against the frame between the foyer and the living room and the small space to the couch. A moment where everything not being his niece meant sat waiting to be acknowledged.

I held my breath, tugging my bottom lip under my teeth. Blood rushed to my cheeks when his eyes dropped to watch the motion.

Say something my body urged. I just didn't know if I wanted him to say something or me.

In the end, it didn't matter.

"Still." He shrugged and turned back to the TV, bringing his own beer to his lips.

Shaking off the moment, I stood back. "I'm gonna change, and then I'll be down."

"Cool."

I fought a smile at the use of his word, which he gave me

shit for overusing the first day.

I threw on a pair of old rolled up boxers and tank top, sighing when I could toss my bra across the room. I didn't consider the consequences of my outfit until I walked in with both hands full of pizza and beer and no way to cover my chest. Thankfully, it was the dark tank and not my thin white one.

Maybe it was the beers he had, but his reaction time was slow, and I couldn't miss the way his eyes dropped to stare at my chest. My nipples hardened, and he swallowed. Heat pooled in my core. Had any man ever really looked at me like that? Like I was water in a desert?

As quick as it started, it ended. He cleared his throat and looked away. "You ever been to Prague?"

"No. But next time for sure."

"Well, dig in and educate yourself for next time."

I sat and devoured my pizza and chugged my beer before falling back against the couch, ready to fall into a coma. When my phone vibrated on the coffee table with my dad's name on the screen, I hit ignore and went back to the show.

"You shouldn't ignore your parents."

"Okay, Dad," I mocked.

"Hey," he held up his hands. "I get it."

"Oh, yeah? Did your parents corner you into who they think you should be?"

"Nah. I'm just saying I get not really wanting to answer to anyone. Even when you know you should pick up the phone. It helps when you finally pick up."

"Speaking from experience?"

He finished off his beer before picking at the label with his thumb. "My mom died shortly after she divorced Harry's dad, and I never knew my dad. I kind of went off the rails and shut everyone out. Including your dad," he admitted, wincing. "He kept calling, and eventually, I picked up. He pulled me back from the edge and encouraged me to get a degree to focus myself. It worked out because I used college as a way to travel abroad as much as I could."

"That sounds like something he'd say."

"Parents aren't always wrong, even when we don't want them to be right."

"Yeah," I sighed. Not wanting to go into anything too deep after a long day, I snuggled down on the couch and curled up to face him. "Tell me your favorite story from traveling."

"Hmmm…" his mouth pinched, and his head tipped to the side. "Probably not my favorite, but a good one was when an entertainer flashed me his balls in Covent Garden."

"No," I gasped.

"Yup." He shuddered, and we both laughed. "Probably one of my favorites was when I went to London for a year of college. On the holidays, I didn't really have anywhere to go and not enough money to fly home even if I wanted to, so a buddy and I rented a van and road tripped through the isles in Scotland. It was cold as fuck, but worth it. Even if I did almost die of hypothermia."

"Oh, my god. Tell me everything," I demanded excitedly.

He huffed a laugh but did as I asked.

Somewhere along the way, I must have fallen asleep because the next morning, he was gone for work, but I woke up covered by a blanket with a pillow tucked under my head.

Imagining Willem tucking me in had me flashing back to my conversation with Felicity, and I couldn't ignore the flash of heat that shot through my limbs. That same heat followed me to the bathroom, where I finally gave in and released the ache with the image of Willem's large, strong body as my muse rushing me to one of my strongest orgasms I've ever had.

FOUR

Willem

THREE DAYS since that night she fell asleep with me still talking. I hadn't noticed, not allowing myself to look over, in fear I'd get caught staring at her chest again. I hadn't noticed until she'd fallen over, her reddish hair bright against my black T-shirt. I'd frozen, not ready to rid myself of the gentle press of her head on my shoulder. Instead, I'd turned the tv off, brushed the hair back from her fair skin, and listened to her soft puffs of breath as my eyes traced the freckles decorating her nose and cheeks.

I'd never seen her without makeup, not that she wore much, but it'd made a difference giving her a more youthful glow. It'd been just the reminder I'd needed in the moment. Her sense of humor and the confidence she exuded just entering a room made me forget she wasn't even twenty.

It'd been then I'd slowly extracted myself. I'd almost made it when she'd sighed and whispered in her sleep, "Tuck me in, Will."

Will.

When was the last time anyone called me Will? It spoke of familiarity and comfort.

A couple friends called me that. Tessa tried to, but I'd hated hearing it in her voice.

But watching the shortened version of my name fall from her perfectly pouty lips shot straight down my spine to my cock like a live wire. Half-sitting half-standing, I'd watched her lips and silently begged to hear it again. I'd stared as images of sliding my dick between the plump curves flooded my brain. I'd almost groaned at the thought of painting them with my cum just to watch her lick it off.

She'd shifted, and I'd finished standing, worried she'd wake to find my hard length tenting my pants. Needing to get away as fast as I could. I'd adjusted her to lay on the couch, firmly keeping my eyes above her neck and covered her with a blanket before practically running upstairs to take a cold shower.

Three days, and I'd taken a cold shower almost every morning and night without even seeing her.

Three days I'd been avoiding her, so I could avoid my attraction.

Three days, and I had every intention of making today the fourth. I just needed to get to the office.

Summer classes wrapped up, but I figured picking up some papers would be the perfect excuse to hide away from her again before the weekend.

I just made it to the stairs when a stranger's voice came from the crack in her door.

"Hang in there, Bella. School will start, and you'll have so many friends, you'll be too busy for measly little me back home."

"Oh, shut up," Arabella said, laughing. "And I know. I just miss you and running to get coffee to chat. I see people at work, but it's not quite the same."

"Go talk to hot Uncle Willem."

I pinched my lips, hiding my laugh at the way her friend said my name in a breathy, seductive voice.

"Shut up. He's not my uncle."

"Your hot uncle."

"Fine, I'll admit to that and nothing else. He's *kind of* hot."

Just for a Little While

"Yesssss."
"Besides, he's been MIA."
"Sorry, boo."
"It's okay. I'll figure it out."
"You always do. But I have to go, Bella. Call me anytime."
"Thank you. Love you."
"Love you, too. Bye."

Guilt had me frozen. Right then, I didn't know what the right thing was. Did I leave to avoid thinking dirty thoughts about my stepbrother's daughter? Or did I stay to help the obviously lonely girl? My shoulders dropped, and I ran a hand over my face. The obvious right thing to do would be to not have *any* illicit thoughts in the first place, but it felt like a useless battle. I could fight all I wanted; they'd just come to me in my dreams anyway.

Making a decision, I knocked on her door and waited.
"Yeah?"
"Can I come in?"
"Yeah."

I pushed the door open to find her sprawled on her bed with her computer in front of her. She wore what looked like a man's flannel shirt that barely allowed the short, frayed hem of her jean shorts to peek out. She closed the laptop, giving me a perfect view of the gaping vee of her shirt, hinting at her cleavage.

"Are you doing anything today?" I asked.

"Ummm..." she hesitated and looked skeptical like I was trying to trick her into something. "No. I just have to work tonight. It's my first Friday," she explained, relaxing her furrowed brows and giving me that devious smirk I've come to know so well. "I'm the beer girl."

"Exciting."

"Hopefully, better tips."

"Well, I was going to see if you wanted to come to school with me today. Classes ended last week, and I needed to grab some papers. I figured I could show you around campus a bit. Maybe get some supplies."

"Umm…"

Her teeth sank into her lush lip, and a hint of regret for asking sank through me. I was just setting myself up for trouble. But she answered before I could even consider backtracking.

"Sure. Let me get changed."

"I'll be downstairs."

Her smirk grew. Not a smile, but still something more. I knew this was a bad idea, but I couldn't regret it too much when she smiled like that.

Surprisingly, conversation was sparse on the way to campus and then on the short walk to my office. She looked around, taking in the tall buildings, her face inscrutable to what she thought of it all.

"So, this is where all the magic happens," she joked, sliding her hand along my desk.

"I guess you could say that," I laughed.

She looked at my diplomas and pictures from my travels I'd displayed on my office walls and shelves as I grabbed my papers.

"Did you know they call you the hottie of economics?"

I groaned and looked up to find her staring at me over her shoulder, her dark brow raised high. "Yeah. I've heard from one or two people. A few students have been a little forward about it, too."

This got her full attention. "Really?"

"Oh, yeah."

She strutted over, somehow making her plain white T-shirt and black denim overalls look sexier than any schoolgirl outfit. When she finally reached my desk, she perched on the edge closest to me. "Thank you, Dr. Deander, for seeing me during office hours," she said in a breathy voice, gently biting on the tip of her finger before running it across her lips. "I'm sure I can earn that A another way now that we have some privacy."

Thank goodness I'd been sitting, otherwise she would have seen what her little performance was doing to me.

"Even the straight A students offer."

"Oh, I bet." She scooted back until her feet dangled above the floor. "The way the girls at work talk about you, they'd take any chance they could with you—for free."

"Jesus," I groaned, both at the thought of anyone gossiping about me and also the way she leaned back on her hands, thrusting her chest out.

"So, Dr. Deander. Would you ever take a student up on her offer?"

"No," I choked. Not because the answer wasn't true, but because I choked down the offer I wanted to make her.

"What if you really...*really* wanted to."

All humor evaporated from the room, her question flooding every square inch with too much tension for anything else. Voices echoed down the hall, but it was as if they couldn't reach us in the bubble we'd created. My hands fisted the arms of my chair, ready to stand and see how serious she was. I wanted to stand in front of her and toe the line. I wanted to see if she'd meet me halfway. I wanted to see if this was all in my mind.

My arms flexed, my body just leaving the chair when the door flung open and in walked Dr. Coven, the head of our department. Her shrewd eyes took in Arabella, leaning back atop my desk, and me leaning back in my chair.

"Dr. Deander. Am I interrupting?" Any heat I'd felt vanished at the chill in her voice. Arabella looked as relaxed as ever.

"Not at all," I managed in a mostly normal voice. "I was just here picking up papers before taking my niece around campus to check it out. She's attending this fall."

Her whole demeanor relaxed as if finally breathing for the first time. "Oh. Good."

"Arabella, this is Dr. Coven. Dr. Coven, Arabella Colins."

Arabella popped down and rounded the desk, hand out. "Nice to meet you."

"You, too, Miss Colins. Will I be seeing you this fall in any economics classes?"

"Most likely not. I'm an education major."

"Well, if anyone can change your mind, it's your uncle."

Thankfully, I was the only one who noticed Arabella's wince at the word uncle. I wanted to wince too, but it was a good reminder of why I shouldn't give in to wanting her.

"I won't keep you from your day. I just heard voices and wanted to stop in and say hello."

"Of course. I'll be here all day Monday."

"Good. I'll see you then. It was nice to meet you, Arabella."

"You too."

Dr. Coven left, and I didn't bother closing the door behind her. I had at least a few more hours with Arabella. If I wanted to survive, I needed to do it with as many watchful eyes as possible.

By the time Arabella needed to get to work, we'd spent more than a few hours together. She'd laughed when I bought us tickets to take the Duck Tour around downtown and into the river.

She moaned when she took her first bite of her Belgian waffle from Taste of Belgium. I'd almost groaned when I watched her lick the syrup and whip cream from her finger.

She'd soaked up every bit of information I shared about Cincinnati like any traveling soul would. I'd loved every minute of sharing my city with her, and I'd had to stop more than once from offering to take her to more cities just so I could experience them through her eyes.

"You gonna make it through the night?" I asked when we pulled up outside the bar.

Just for a Little While

"I think I can make do. I'll do a few shots and be fine."

"What?" I almost shouted like a concerned parent.

"Kidding, Dad. I'll probably pound a Red Bull and make it through with sheer willpower."

"A solid plan. Thanks for hanging out with this old man today."

"Anytime, Grandpa."

"Ugh, that's worse than dad."

"You don't like it when I call you daddy?"

I gave her my most deadpan stare.

"Fine, Uncle Will."

"Jesus Christ," I groaned.

Her laugh followed her out of the car. Before she walked inside, I rolled down the window.

"Hey. What time are you off?"

She whirled around, her hair like a fiery halo. "Midnight."

"I'll be here before then to take you home."

"You don't have to do that."

"I know. I want to."

Her lips shifted slightly—not into a smirk, but an endearing smile. She looked genuinely happy without any mirth.

"Thank you."

"Anytime. See you then."

I waited until she disappeared behind the doors and went home, counting down the minutes until I could see her again, kicking myself the whole time for how far I'd fallen today.

I'd fallen straight into *completely fucked* territory.

FIVE

Arabella

"Holy. Shit. My fantasy is coming to life."

I looked up to find Amber's wide eyes directed toward the door. Jerking around, I half expected Channing Tatum to walk in, eyes glued to her. Instead, I found Willem with his hair slicked back, in a dark T-shirt and black jeans, looking ten times more relaxed than the slacks and button up from earlier today. He looked side-to-side before grabbing a seat at one of the high-tops close to the bar.

"Dr. Deander is actually here," she squealed. "How do I look? Do my boobs look okay?" she asked, rearranging them in her bra for full effect.

In all honesty, her boobs did look great, and jealousy fired through me before I could tame it.

"Umm, yeah. But he's not like that."

"Shh," she reprimanded, not taking her eyes off him. "Let me dream."

The problem was that I'd begun dreaming about him and couldn't seem to stop. I sure as hell didn't want to know anyone else was dreaming about him too.

"Amber," Xander called from the bar. "Your drinks are ready."

"Dammit," she whined, wincing when she finally peeled her eyes off Willem like it physically hurt her to stop. I kind of understood. "Stupid work. Maybe I'll just drop by one of his classes."

"Aren't you a design major?"

"Yeah." She shrugged. "But economics is good for that. I can learn fashion trends through the economy."

"I...don't think that's how it works."

"Fine," she sighed. "I'll just have to hope he notices me here then. Although, that won't happen with the way women flock to him."

I whirled around to find a dark-haired woman leaning into Willem's space, dragging her finger down his arm. If I thought I was jealous of Amber's boobs, it was nothing compared to the raging inferno flooding my veins now.

"I—I should go check on him. Grab him a beer."

Without waiting for an answer, I weaved through the crowd, grabbed his favorite beer, and made my way to his table.

"Hey, Will. I brought you your favorite."

Did I smile as I used the shortened version of his name for a personal effect? Yup.

Did I quickly change that smile to my trademark snotty smirk when I faced the busty brunette next to him? Also, yup.

Did I feel victory when he did a double-take at my outfit change? Hell yes.

I'd ditched the white T-shirt under my overalls and just had on my black bralette. It managed to be cute, sexy, and stylish all at once.

"*Will?*" she sneered, looking from me to him like she'd caught him cheating. "Who is this, Willem?"

Obviously, she wasn't privy to calling him Will.

Willem gave me a look that let me know he knew what I was doing. A hint of laughter sparking behind his light eyes and the slight twitch to his lips let me know he didn't mind either.

"This is my niece, Arabella. Arabella, this is Tessa."

"Oh." Her entire demeanor changed. "Hi. It's so nice to meet some of his family."

She was beaming, clearly viewing me as the ticket to getting in deeper with Willem.

"Nice to meet you," manners had me saying. But my smile never changed.

When I didn't say anything more, her smile faltered and she cleared her throat, turning her attention back on Willem. "Like I said, I hadn't expected to see you here, but now that you are, maybe we can have a drink. I'm just here with some friends. They wouldn't mind."

Willem looked to his watch, which I knew let him know I was off in fifteen minutes. He met my eyes as if looking for something. Permission to leave me here to walk home so he could go fuck her? Help on getting out of the situation? I wasn't sure, so I kept my gaze blank and steady, intrigued to see what he did.

"Tonight's not a good night."

I hadn't realized until he said the words that I'd been holding my breath. The air in my lungs rushed out. My tense muscles relaxing in relief.

"Oh. Okay." Tessa looked down before pulling herself together again. She leaned in close, pressing her breasts against his arm and rested her hand on his chest, whispering something in his ear.

Willem's face didn't change in the slightest, not giving me a hint as to what she said. She dragged her hand across his chest and bicep when she walked away.

"She seems nice."

He drained his beer. "She is."

"Why didn't you take her up on her offer?"

"Because I said I'd give you a ride home."

"I could walk."

"Yeah, but I didn't want to go back on my word. Also, I'm just not interested."

Why? I wanted to ask, but bit back. I knew what I wanted his answer to be. Lately, my dreams had gotten away from me. They no longer crept in at night only. I'd find myself thinking of him throughout the day. I didn't know if it was because I was bored or what, but my mind went wild, and in that moment, I wanted him to look at me and say he turned her down because he was interested in me.

"Either way. Thanks for not leaving me." He nodded but didn't say anything else. "You want another one?"

"Nah. I'm good. However, I am interested in knowing what the hell happened to your shirt."

"Do you not like it?" I posed for effect, barely holding back my laugh at watching him flounder over an answer.

"It's not that I—It's just that—I—" He dragged a hand over his face. "It's a little revealing."

"I'm the beer girl. Gets me more tips if I show a little skin." His jaw clenched under his scruff, and I enjoyed watching him struggle, so I asked again, turning side to side. "Do you not like it?"

His mouth opened and closed as he struggled to not look at my naked sides. Honestly, it wasn't that revealing. The overalls came above my boobs. However, the lace bra left my sides bare and gave the illusion of being more naked than I actually was.

Another girl came up to his side, saving him from answering.

"Hi," she greeted, mixing false shyness with full seduction. "I saw you from my seat and wanted to know if you wanted to dance."

"Oh, thank you, but no. I'm just here to pick up my niece."

Her eyes flicked to me like she somehow missed my existence. "Okay." She shrugged but didn't turn down the heat in her eyes. "If you change your mind, I'm just over there."

When she walked away, a laugh slipped free.

"What?" he grumbled.

"Uncle Will is a player."

He cringed.

"What?"

"Nothing. And I'm just a man. I can't control that women approach me."

"So, you're saying you're just waiting for the right girl? That if I wasn't here, you wouldn't have taken either of them up on their offer?"

"I can't say because you are here."

"Oh, come on. I bet either one would let you fuck them before even leaving."

"Jesus, Arabella."

"What? There's no shame in it. Do you have hoes in different area codes?" I kept joking as he laughed, pushing my luck for a reaction. "I bet you would take them to the bathroom."

"Christ. Stop, please," he groaned.

"Bella," Xander shouted from the bar. "You're off for the night."

"Thank God," he sighed.

"What? Can't handle turning another hottie down?"

He glared with no heat. "Go grab your stuff and let's head home."

When we got home, I was too keyed up to sleep. "I think I'm going to watch a movie. I'm not quite ready for bed yet."

"Want some company?" he asked.

"Sure."

As if adrenaline hadn't already flooded my system after joking with Willem at the bar, the chance to sit and watch a movie with him had me practically running high. I tossed on my typical PJs, grappling with the decision of bra or no bra. Feeling reckless, I went with no bra and did my best to walk down the stairs instead of run.

"I figured some chips and beer would help settle you down."

"Perfect."

And it was. Him sprawled on the couch in lounge pants and

another tight T-shirt clinging to his broad chest. He looked like just the company I wanted to end my night with.

"What are you smiling about?"

"Nothing. Just excited about our movie."

"You don't even know what I picked."

I didn't have another excuse ready for why my smirk had gone missing to be replaced by my giddy smile, so I settled on a shrug and tucked in. He thankfully didn't push.

The movie ended up being the first Avengers, which we soon realized our love of Marvel was another thing we had in common. We talked about our favorite parts and characters and had a few more beers.

"You know, this is nice," I said when the credits started rolling.

"What?"

"Just...sitting here." I picked at the label on my beer, the condensation soaking through the leg of my shorts as I thought over my words. "My parents were always gone, either working or at an event for work. I didn't love being alone all the time, so I hung out with friends, which led to me always having to be... on. I don't have to be when it's just Felicity and me, but it's rarely just us. When everyone else is around, they have these expectations of who you are, and you kind of just fall into it, and the whole time feels superficial and fake. So, it's nice to just *be* with someone. I guess I didn't get enough of it at home."

"My mom was busy a lot, too. But she always made time for me. And I grew up in a different generation than you. We didn't have the pressures and influence of social media quite like you do. It definitely adds a layer. Almost like a veneer that protects the outside world from who you really are."

"Yeah. And I didn't even get to let that veneer down with my parents. Like, I knew they loved me. Or at least that they wanted to. They just want me to be someone I'm not, and I think it's hard to love me when they're also disappointed in who I actually am." As if the trickling of truth led to a crack that spread wider, the words flooded out. "I don't know. I guess they just had so many expectations and they forgot to be affectionate parents. You know, the few people I got hugs from was Grandpa and Felicity. But they're not the same."

"Nothing is quite like a mom hug," Willem admitted. "I think it's the one thing I miss the most about her are her hugs. She had the stereotypical mom hug and there's nothing like it. And as you get older, a hug is a less common thing to get from someone."

"You don't cuddle all your hoes in different area codes?" I joked.

He thankfully laughed, but it held a tinge of sadness with it. "No. I haven't had a serious girlfriend in a while and hugs are usually quick and impersonal."

"Exactly."

We both leaned back on the couch, staring at the black screen, silently lost in what we were missing.

An idea hit me, and maybe it was the three beers, but I didn't think twice. I jumped from the couch and stood in front of him, my hands reaching for his. "Give me your hands. Stand up."

His brows furrowed, but he did as I ordered and let me pull him up. The rough scrape of his palms on mine almost shocked me frozen, and I realized it was the first time we'd actually touched. I wanted to stop and take in every new sensation of his hands in mine, but I had a plan, and I didn't want to stop. If all went well, we'd be touching a lot more than just palms.

"I want to try something."

"Ummm...okay," he said slowly.

Stepping in closer, I realized how much shorter I was than him, and I wanted as much contact as possible. Regretfully, I let go of his hands and used his shoulders to steady myself as I climbed onto the couch. I wobbled, and his hands shot out to my hips to steady me. Electricity shot from his grip to my core and up my chest, jolting my heart.

Focus, Bella.

"What are you—"

His words cut off when I jerked him against me and wrapped my arms around his neck, pressing as much of myself against him as I could. His grip tightened, but he stood in my arms like a statue.

"Arabella," he whispered as if afraid someone would hear and come see. "Wha—"

"Shhh. Just for a little while."

I hugged him tighter, spreading my hand along his strong back, burying my head against his shoulder. It only took a moment for him to give in. His hands moved from my hips, up my back, pulling me close.

The seconds ticked by, and the hug grew more intense. Our fingers dug into each other's flesh. Our heads burrowed in each other's shoulders. We stood chest to chest, legs to legs, every inch we could reach pressed tight as if trying to absorb each other's strength—as if trying to fortify ourselves for another long stretch of no more hugs.

Somewhere in the moments, the hug shifted and became less about comfort and more heated. His hot breath brushed against the skin of my neck like I wished his lips would. I turned my head into his neck and inhaled his citrus scent, barely holding back from tasting him. His hand coasted up and down my back, still digging in and holding tight, almost pulling a pleasured moan from my lips.

My heart stalled and threatened to plummet to my feet when he pulled back, but instead of stopping, he merely shifted and sat in the corner of the couch, tugging me down with him to his side.

Without a word, his arm wrapped around my shoulders. Unsure of what was happening, but unwilling to ask, I lifted my chin to look up.

His dark eyes locked with mine.

A million words passed between us without mouths even moving.

This isn't just about a hug.
This isn't about comfort.
This is wrong.
I'm not ready to stop.
I don't want to.

Instead of all that, he only said one thing and it was enough.
"Just for a little while."

SIX

Arabella

I STROLLED DOWN THE HALL, scrolling the latest on Instagram in one hand and finishing off my popsicle in the other. I was so lost in Todd's latest eye-roll-worthy post that I missed the key in the lock. So, when the door swung open, I jerked my gaze up in time to take in Willem walking through the door, the sunny day backlighting him like some god.

"Hey," he greeted, closing the door.

When he turned, our eyes met, and I stood frozen, letting him take me in from my head to my teal toenail polish. My cut-off shorts and over-sized tank top, sans bra, covered not enough and too much all at once.

He'd left early for work this morning, so we hadn't talked since the quiet, strained goodnight we gave in the hallway after our hug. We'd both said just for a little while, but we didn't give a limit on how many, and taking in his broad chest straining the limits of his black polo, all I could think about was getting my arms around him again.

Testing the waters, I walked over, setting my phone and popsicle stick on the entryway table before facing him. The quiet hum of cars driving by and birds chirping crept in from outside, but it was almost impossible to hear over the silence screaming around us. We both stood still, like two gun-slingers before a duel, until I cracked and closed the gap. As soon as my arms cleared his shoulders, he dropped his bag with a thud and held me close.

I wanted to sigh in relief that he hadn't turned me away. I'd started the hug last night for him, but once his arms surrounded me, I knew I needed it too.

Two large palms splayed across my back, pulling me almost too tight, and yet, I took my first deep breath of the day. I raised as high as I could on my toes and buried my head in his neck.

"Welcome home," I whispered.

His fingers flexed, and a thrill of excitement shot through me. I loved that I affected him—that I could tell I affected him.

"Damn, you give good hugs for such a tiny girl," he rumbled, the words vibrating against my chest.

I inched back enough to meet his eyes, and he loosened his grip, lowering me back to the ground. My brow cocked at the *tiny girl* comment.

"How about a petite woman?" I corrected, smiling, dying a little when he smiled back.

"Fair enough."

His hands relaxed from around my back, slowly sliding down only to grip my hips while I left my hands on his shoulders. We looked like a couple of grade-school kids at a dance, and I'd take every second of it.

Deciding to push my luck, I asked, "Do you want to watch TV for a bit?"

He looked down to his bag on the floor, probably filled with paperwork needing to be done. In fact, I remembered him mentioning how bogged down he was with prepping for a new course, and I cringed, wanting to take it back to save me the misery of being turned down.

Digging my teeth into my bottom lip, I braced for the impact of rejection when instead he said, "Just for a little while."

And that's how almost every day over the next week

Just for a Little While

progressed—when either of us walked through the door, we greeted each other with a hug that became more natural each day. Sometimes we'd watch TV on the couch. Sometimes I'd even curl up close to him—every time with the simple promise of just for a little while.

But on Saturday, neither of us had to work, and Mother Nature made staying inside much more preferable than going out into the storms. We lounged in shorts and T-shirts, blasting the air conditioning to combat the humidity seeping into the house. When that still didn't work, we decided to say fuck it and do a little day-drinking. He ordered a pizza, and I grabbed the beers.

"Just one," he muttered.

"Okay, I'll remind you of that later when you want another." I played dumb, smiling innocently.

He gave a deadpanned stare with narrowed eyes, and I laughed. "Okay, Dad. I'll try not to get trashed on your couch."

With a roll of his eyes, he plopped down beside me, flipping open a delicious box of mushroom, onion, and sausage pizza.

"Since you got to pick the pizza, I get to pick the show," he declared.

"Ugh, fine," I said around my too-big-bite. Not that I really minded, because he always picked something good.

In the end, he settled on a documentary about ancient Rome.

"Did you ever see Rome?" he asked.

"No. I wanted to, but the only time it worked out was in peak tourist season, and I'd rather wait than fight through the crowds in the heat."

"It's a beautiful city, but less enjoyable in the heat. I went twice, and visiting in the spring was much better than summer."

"Duly noted." I pretended to jot it down on an imaginary paper and shove it in my pocket. He laughed at my antics before turning to the show, leaving me to stare at him. His smile really transformed him and called to me. I rarely smirked at him anymore, instead offering up genuine happiness.

Eventually, the show pulled my attention away from him—at least a little. When he grabbed another beer, he brought another back for me with a look that said any smart comment would result in said beer being taken away. I mimed zipping my lips, but as the alcohol worked its way through my veins, I relaxed and decided to push my limits.

Slowly, I adjusted, inching my way closer to close the barely-there gap between us. Resituating this way and that until I leaned over enough to rest my head on his shoulder. He stiffened for less than a second before shifting, allowing me access to fully curl into his side.

As if to add normalcy to the situation, he started quizzing me on my opinions of each historical fact the show shared. We debated the pros and cons of Rome's society as a whole and moved on to Greece when those episodes played next. All of it held a platonic vibe—minus the way my side was pressed to his. Or the way our eyes dropped to each other's lips when I turned to face him, only to be inches away.

I found myself searching for the most absurd questions just for the excuse to turn and look up at him and burn under his eyes on my mouth. My lips tingled, and each time I shifted, I imagined it was the time I'd give in to the desire to find out what the beer tasted like from his lips—on his tongue. I imagined it'd be the time he gave in and took what I so obviously offered.

Need coiled around every muscle, and when the next show discussed the sexuality in Athens, I was sure I'd explode. Each mention of dominance and the open freedom of the culture pushed me closer and closer to the edge. His questions stopped, and he became stoically quiet, making me want to poke and prod to see if I could get a reaction out of him—hopefully, one that led to his mouth on mine.

When the show talked about how uncommon it was to kiss

your partner in Athens, I found my opening. "I could never imagine not kissing."

He cleared his throat before responding. "Why's that?"

I smirked at his graveled tone, imagining him struggling like me. Because this couldn't be one-sided. I refused to believe I was the only one standing on this precipice.

"It's just too good. The connection. The passion."

I looked up, disappointed when I didn't find him staring back like he had all the other times I'd asked him anything. But I didn't fall back. Instead, I traced the sharp line of his brow and cheek, visible even under his scruff. I mapped every visible inch before he finally—slowly—turned to face me.

His eyes dropped to my lips, and I slid my tongue across, flicking my gaze to his mouth before looking back to meet his deep blue eyes.

In my imagination, he stood on the cliff with me, staring out over the abyss. I wanted to jump, but I wanted him to jump with me.

"What's your favorite kind of kiss? A peck?" I offered, throwing out more suggestions. "Long and lingering? Sweet?"

"Aggressive," he growled like a promise. "Tasting. Controlling."

Oh, God. I almost moaned—almost climbed onto his lap and demanded he show me. Somehow, I managed to hold back—at least a little. I approached with caution, holding my breath and flexing my muscles to shift a fraction of an inch closer.

I stood on the cliff, him by my side, and I held out my hand for him to take what he wanted.

He leaned down, preparing to take my hand and jump with me.

Only one more inch—one more breath.

Until the loud ring of the doorbell brought reality crashing all around us. As if a bucket of cold water slapped him back to reality, he froze and literally jumped at the chance to put distance between us.

Dammit. I wanted to scream. I wanted to fling myself back against the couch, stomp my feet, and punch my fists against the sofa in frustration.

So close, only to be stopped by some solicitor, probably.

Taking a deep breath, I tried to pull myself together for when he came back. We had all night, and I'd use every second to get us to where we were.

At least until Willem greeted our visitor and a whole fucking tidal wave of cold water dumped over me.

"Harry. Hey. What are you doing here?" Willem asked.

Freaking Harry.

AKA—my dad.

SEVEN

Willem

I LOOKED into the familiar brown eyes I'd known for years. Harry smiled, bringing a light to his gaze that reminded me of the light that had sparked in Arabella's moments ago.

I gripped the door handle, hating myself because while this man I looked up to and owed so much to greeted me like family, all I could think about was how seconds ago I'd almost taught his daughter how a man like me kissed and what that kissing led to afterward.

Fuck. Fuck. Fucking fuck.

"Sorry," I sputtered, shaking the thoughts from my head and stepping back. "Where are my manners? Come in."

Harry waved my apology away and walked inside from the rain. "No need to apologize. I'm sure your brother from across the country showing up randomly would throw anyone."

I took his dripping coat and turned just in time to find Arabella standing there with a towel stretched out for her father. I said a silent prayer of thanks when I noticed she put on a T-shirt that covered her a lot more than the tank top from earlier.

Not that we had anything to hide.

Because nothing had happened.

Or would have happened.

Yeah, right. Like you weren't less than a second away from finally feasting from her mouth.

"Hey, Dad. Long time no see. You could have just called rather than flown here to check on me."

"Well, here's the thing about phones, Arabella," he said, taking the towel. "In order for them to work, someone needs to pick up."

Arabella's jaw dropped, giving a look of false wonder. "Ohhhh. See, I never knew that. They must have forgot to teach me that in school. Thankfully, I'm going to college for that kind of knowledge."

Harry huffed a laugh and shook his head. "Still so snarky," he muttered, pulling her in for an awkward side hug. "Thank goodness I love you."

She gave him a pat on the back in return but pulled back quickly.

"Anyway, I was on my way to a conference in New York when we hit this storm, and we had to land. As luck would have it, we landed here, but we're delayed until tomorrow morning."

"You could have called me. I would have come get you."

"Well, here's the thing about phones, Willem..." he started with a smirk that let me know where Arabella got it from.

"I pick up my phone," I grumbled, patting my pockets and coming up empty. "At least when I have it on me." I rolled my eyes and went to grab my phone from where it fell out of my pocket into the couch cushions. Sure enough, one missed call.

"So, how are things going?" Harry asked, looking between Arabella and me. "Has her bitterness over coming to college drove you insane yet? Do I need to take her home with me?"

Arabella forced a smile, crossing her arms like she was trying to defend herself against his barbed joke. When she dropped her gaze to her bare feet, I saw the girl who avoided phone calls from her parents, not because she was bratty, but because their disapproval hurt.

"It's actually been great. She's a phenomenal house guest."

Just for a Little While

Harry's brows shot up, looking to me like I told him she wore fifties dresses and packed my lunch every day. His gaze shot to Arabella, but she was too busy looking at me. I offered a small smile, trying to hide how much the way her jaw relaxed into a soft curve of wonder affected me. Had no one stood up for her before?

"We were actually just binging the History Channel together, trading stories about our travels."

"That's right. You know, I thought about how much you two have in common, but I figured Arabella would be out gallivanting with friends too much to stay home and get to know you. At home, she appeared to eat and sleep and was off again."

"I was home more than that. You just weren't there to notice," she muttered.

Halting any reaction to that comment before it could start, I kept talking. "I'm much cooler than any of those hipsters."

"No one says hipsters anymore, Uncle Will."

I glared at the Uncle Will comment, not missing the slight twitch in her lips. "I'm bringing it back," I explained.

She gave a thumbs up, finally relaxing her arms from around herself. "Good luck with that."

Harry watched our banter and shook his head. He scanned the room, landing on the two beer bottles on the table. Thankfully, one was empty, so it could be passed off as both of them being mine. Before he could comment, I quickly suggested dinner.

The night progressed with food and a Marvel movie. Apparently, Arabella got her love of the world from Harry. Thankfully, the tension eased a bit, the sharp-edged jokes becoming less and less. The ones that did come, I did my best to deflect without drawing too much attention as to why I wanted to protect her so much.

Mainly because if someone asked me, I wasn't sure I could explain. This past week of hugs had built something slowly—something more than physical attraction. It wove its way around us, tying me to her in a way I wasn't sure I wanted to evaluate too closely. When it prodded my thoughts, I shoved it down as just appreciation for the simple affection.

Yeah, that was it.

By the time we called it a night, my body ached at the thought of going to bed without at least one more hug from her. But having her father in the house made it damn near impossible to ignore everything that was wrong with what we were doing. It made it difficult to explain it away as just a simple hug we didn't have to explain. Outside eyes gave us another perspective, shining a light on the things we tried to ignore.

So, after setting Harry up on the couch, I forced myself to walk past her room toward mine. My muscles clenched, fighting each step, but I made it to the other side of my door and locked it. What I needed was a lock to keep me inside.

Especially because almost an hour later, I laid awake in bed, staring up at the moon streaking across my ceiling. Harry stopped talking about forty minutes ago, and I assumed he had gone to sleep.

I hoped so because my muscles won out.

I flung the covers back and quietly, but quickly, crept down the hall and tried to stop my knuckles from making contact with the wood door but failed.

Holding my breath, listening for any slight sound from downstairs, I tapped against her door. Part of me hoped she didn't answer, that she fell asleep hours ago when she made excuses to go to bed earlier. The other part begged and pleaded that she open the door and wrap her arms around me.

In those seconds of waiting, I realized how far down the rabbit hole I'd fallen. Besides the fact that she was my stepbrother's daughter. Besides the fact that she was nineteen. Besides the fact that she'd be a student at the college I taught at. Besides all of that, I think I was most alarmed at how I couldn't get to sleep without one more embrace in her arms. Like I needed them to hold me together and patch me up for a little bit longer.

The dependency worried me the most.

But I didn't get a chance to think about it because the latter hopeful part was answered, and the door flung open.

With the blink of an eye, Arabella's small body crashed into mine, and I let go of the tension I'd been holding with my breath. I slid my palms around her back and buried myself in her hair, losing myself for the moment in the vanilla scent encompassing us.

For just a little while—just a second—I allowed myself to imagine picking her up and carrying her back to my bed to hold onto all night. As quickly as it came, I shoved it away.

Nonsense. Dangerous, pointless nonsense.

Slowly, I forced myself to relax my grip and ease back. Before I could, she squeezed me tight one more time, turning her mouth toward my ear.

"Goodnight, Will."

Shivers raced down my spine from the graze of her breath on my skin.

"Goodnight, Arabella."

And with that, I let go, turning back to my room without looking at her. I was too scared that if I met her eyes in that moment, it'd be like staring into a mirror and facing everything I didn't want to face.

Like how holding back from her felt like a losing battle.

It didn't matter.

I had to try.

EIGHT

Willem

"What the hell is that?"

"Wow, that was an impressive pitch for a man your size."

"Arabella," I growled this time.

"A dress?"

"I can see your underwear."

She rolled her eyes like the teen she was. "It's not my underwear. Although I guess it could be since I'm not wearing any under it."

"Jesus Christ, save me." It looked like a high-waisted bathing suit under a black sheer skirt with red dots all over it. "You look like you're wearing a bikini."

"It's obviously not a bikini. It has sleeves." She stretched her arms out, fully exposing her bare stomach. The sleeves she spoke of attached to something that looked like a strapless bra, made of the same sheer material as her skirt.

When I continued to gawk, she gave another eye roll and a sigh for good measure.

"Where are you going? School starts in two days."

"I'm aware, Dad. That's why a few of us from the bar are heading to Over the Rhine."

"Where in OTR?

"I don't know. Amber just said some bars."

I rubbed a hand over my face, and she snickered, knowing it was a sure sign of my stress. "Just be careful. There's a fine line between trendy and dangerous down there."

"We'll be fine. Xander is coming too and promised to keep an eye on us."

I fucking bet he did. He probably planned to keep an extra close eye on Arabella.

"Call me if you need me."

"Will do. Don't wait up."

And with a swoosh of fabric and red hair, she was gone.

It'd been two weeks since the night Arabella hugged me the first time, and we walked our own dangerous line every day.

On the nights she worked, I went in for a beer fifteen minutes before she got off and drove her home. In that time span, I'd grow more and more agitated watching Xander flirt with her. By the time she got off, I was ready to shut out the world and be alone.

We'd come home and almost as soon as we walked through the door, we were in each other's arms, holding on tight, one of us whispering our promise.

Just for a little while.

When we finally let go, we'd get changed and meet on the couch to watch a movie or a travel show. Between commercials, we'd share stories of our own adventures. We'd start with a couple feet between us, but by the end, we'd made our way together. Her tucked close to my side.

We knew it was wrong, but it was as if we didn't speak of it, we could ignore just how wrong it was.

Watching her walk out to go be with friends—especially Xander—had me on edge. It'd be the first night she wasn't home with me, and while I wanted her to have her fun and be independent, I missed her.

Also, fucking Xander was there.

Just the thought of him dancing with her and possibly taking her home had jealousy burning up my throat.

After the third show of me staring at the screen, taking nothing in, I grabbed my phone. I considered calling Tessa to take my mind off of Arabella. Maybe I needed to remove the temptation or put my desires elsewhere to save us from the edge.

Before I opened my contacts, I opened Instagram. Just out of curiosity, I tapped Arabella's profile and saw the red circle around her picture. Holding my breath, I tapped the image. First to come up was a meme. Next was a picture of her sitting on the iconic white buildings of Greece looking out over the water with the hashtag, Santorini Saturday. I almost gave up when her final story was a video of her dancing with one of the blondes from work. The camera shifted closer and bounced for a bit before flipping to selfie mode, and Xander's face filled the screen, turning it on him coming up behind Arabella to dance with her.

Without thought, I closed the phone and shot up, grabbing my keys and heading out.

I recognized the bar and hoped they hadn't moved since the video had been posted. Otherwise, I might as well slap on a robe and curlers and hunt down my child like a crazy person.

Fuck. I'd already delved headfirst into crazy. But walking into Japp's, I didn't care.

I especially didn't care when I spotted her red hair piled on top of her head toward the back. Amber and Gia sat on one side and Arabella on the other. The other two stood out, but Arabella's vintage confidence blended in with the old-time design.

My steps slowed, and I hesitated. She almost smiled and looked more relaxed than I'd seen her. She looked happy.

I stopped, ready to turn back when Amber saw me.

"Oh my god, Dr. Deander," she squealed.

Arabella's head whipped my way. Even though her eyes widened, her mouth softened to an actual smile. More than the

Just for a Little While

smirk she gave everyone else, but less than the laugh I knew she was capable of.

The girls waved me over, and every second of my thirty-three years weighed on me as I loomed over this young table. I assumed the other girls were over twenty-one since they had a colorful drink in hand except for Arabella. The two blondes who looked freakishly similar also had matching glassy eyes and flushed cheeks.

"Hello, ladies."

"Hey, Dr. D. Can I call you Dr. D?"

"Sure," I laughed. Looking around the group, I noticed one missing. "Where's Xander?" I asked Arabella.

"Probably picking up that chick that followed us from Motor," one of the blondes answered, rolling her eyes.

"Oh my god, how lucky are you, Bella, to have Dr. D as your uncle," the other cut in before I could ask anything else.

"So lucky," she deadpanned. Neither of the girls heard the sarcasm in her voice.

"I mean, if you ever wanted to do a sleepover, I'd totally be down," one of them said, looking up at me and swaying in her seat.

"You're such a slut, Amber," the other giggled.

I wondered if Arabella knew she was openly scowling at the two girls.

"Do you want to dance, Dr. D?" Amber asked, completely unperturbed by her friend's insult.

"Oh, no, thank you. I appreciate the offer. I just happened to come down here for a drink. It's a coincidence I ran into you. I don't want to interrupt Arabella's night out before school."

Arabella's head tipped to one side, and I wondered what was going through her mind. Did she think I was a stalker? I kind of felt like one. She left for a night out, and there I was showing up too.

Her face looked like a placid lake, showing zero emotion beyond curiosity.

"Oh, Bella is having fun. You're totally not interrupting. I never knew she was such a good dancer."

"I didn't know either," I admitted.

Her gaze dropped to the clear liquid in her tall glass, which I hoped was water, and doubt hit me harder than before. I'd have expected her to lift her chin higher and make some comment about how she was the best damn dancer there. Instead, she looked away, and I missed her curious stare from moments before.

Despite that, I still wasn't ready to leave.

"I'm just going to grab a drink at the bar. Enjoy your night."

She glanced up, but her dark golden eyes gave nothing away.

I promised myself just one beer to make my reasons look valid, and then I'd head home.

I chatted with the bartender, the entire time keeping my eye on Arabella. A few glances over let me know she kept her eyes on me too. However, so did the girls with a lot less subtlety.

I'd almost finished my beer when a Black Keys song came on, and all three stood up, moving to the small dance floor. At first, I tried not to openly stare, but soon my glances grew longer. One song bled into another, and I learned first-hand, that Amber was right, Arabella was a good dancer.

Her body swayed with the beat in an effortless sexy way. The sheer material of her skirt like a curtain you wanted to shove out of the way to watch the full show of her strong legs. The smooth skin of her stomach flexed with each roll and twist. Her tits bouncing with her arms lifted high.

I fought to look away—to not stare, until she turned, her eyes locking on mine and any lack of emotions before vanished. Instead of placid curiosity, fire burned across the space between us. Her eyes demanded I watch her—watch the show she put on. For me.

Her lips parted, her tongue peeking out to slick across the rosy bottom curve. Her hands slid down her body, back up past her breasts and around her neck. My hands clenched, aching to follow the same path.

The songs bled together, and even from my perch on the stool, I could see the sheen to her skin, desperate to taste it.

Maybe it was because we were out of the house. Maybe it was because we were just tired of pretending. Maybe it was that the ten feet between us made it feel safe, but all pretenses fell away, and we let the desire we both held back flood the room.

"Would you like another, sir?" the bartender asked.

Would I? Yeah. I could sit there all night watching her. But then Xander stepped into view, coming up behind her, and I swear, the music scratched. She faltered for a moment but met my eyes again and started dancing. Almost like a challenge. A challenge I couldn't answer in the middle of a public bar.

A challenge, I shouldn't ever answer.

"No, thank you."

I dropped a ten into the tip jar and walked past Arabella to the back. I tried not to look at her, tried not to issue my own challenge as I passed, but failed. Our eyes locked, and the half a second froze time, and a million wants and needs tore between us.

I rounded two corners before I found a semi-private corner to catch my breath. I should have gone into the bathroom rather than walking past. I should have walked out the front door and not looked back, but I wasn't ready for it to end just yet.

"I thought you left," her soft voice brought my eyes up.

"Just taking a piss."

She stood three feet away, and I tried to use crassness to hold her back. A useless effort since she closed the distance with slow, measured steps. The world shrunk to a bubble around us, the thump of the music beyond nothing but an echo matching my heartbeat.

"Why are you here, Willem?"

Less than a foot away, and I did my best to swallow it down and choke out part of the truth. "I just wanted to check on you and have a drink out. Been a while since I've been down here." Her trademark smirk called bullshit. "Have you been drinking?"

"No. Just having some fun with friends." While I stood leaning against the wall, hoping it would hold me in place and stop me from taking her like I craved, she prowled closer, chin high, sexual strength pouring off every inch of her as she cornered me. "Want to dance?"

"Arabella," I warned.

"Come on." Her hands slid to my hips before moving up my chest. "Just for a little while."

Her fingers scraped across my shoulders and down my arms as she swayed side to side. My hands remained pressed to the wall, my willpower the only glue keeping me steady.

When she turned and pressed her ass against my groin, the first fracture formed in my weak resolve. She dropped low and straightened her legs first before rolling her back up.

In this darkened hallway, she danced for me like she hadn't danced for anyone else. My own private performance. She stood and looked over her shoulder, that perfect lip that taunted me even before she arrived, buried under her straight teeth.

Crack.

Any strength I had to hold back, broke.

She thought she was stronger than me. That she would be the one to control the situation.

She had no idea what I was capable of, but I was damn well ready to show her.

I gripped her hips and switched our positions, slamming her against the wall.

She winced when her back hit the wall, but I couldn't step back. "Did I hurt you?" I asked, looking her over, down her body, growing harder to find her nipples pressing against the thin material of her top.

"No," she answered, leaning up to my ear to whisper, "I liked it."

"Fuck." My hands fisted against the wall, caging her in, maybe some small semblance holding me back.

Some pinch of sanity telling me not to fuck a nineteen-year-old in the back hallway of a bar. Her hands rubbed up and down my chest, over my shoulders and around my neck, pulling me in for what we'd done almost every day, but making it so very different.

Her hug was anything but comfort and everything like a tortured sexual tease. Her soft tongue flicked my ear before whispering, "Just for a little while."

Without pushing her back because I didn't want to part from her, I growled, "We're leaving."

"What?" she almost shrieked, jerking back, hurt marring every part of her face.

She didn't understand.

But she would.

My inactive hands snapped into action, one gripping her hip hard and the other framing her jaw, not giving her a chance to look away. "We're. Leaving. Now follow me and get in the car. We're going home."

"But—"

I pressed my hard cock against her stomach, grinding on her, leaving no room to miss what I wanted. "Now."

With that last order, I walked away, praying she followed.

With every step, I knew with certainty that this was a mistake. With every step, I knew I didn't care.

It would be like everything else.

I could plead insanity.

Just for a little while.

NINE

Arabella

THE DOOR SLAMMED BEHIND ME, and I whipped around, backing away slower than Willem prowled toward me.

I wanted to be caught, but I enjoyed the chase too.

My back hit the banister, and I looked side to side. Up the stairs to the bedroom or over to the living room. My mind quickly flashed with visions of what his stare promised. Each position more deviant than the last.

When he stood less than an arm's length away, I twisted to the side and tried to run up the stairs, but he was faster. He snatched my wrist and whirled me around to the wall by the steps like he had at the bar and blocked my escape. Except this time, he didn't hold back. He didn't fist his hands in resistance on either side of my head. No. He followed with intention, and before I could blink, his mouth was on mine.

I didn't hesitate. I pressed to my toes, adding to the pressure of the kiss. My hands gripped his waist and tugged him to meet me halfway, groaning at the hard length pressing to my stomach. His kiss was as hard as him. The thick scruff surrounding his lips abraded my skin and smeared my lipstick. I knew I looked a mess, but I didn't care. I wanted him to eat me up and make a mess of every inch of me. Just so I could turn around and do the same to him.

His teeth dug into my bottom lip, pulling a shocked gasp from me.

"I've wanted to do that since I opened the door to you chewing on it."

"What took you so long?" I taunted.

"Goddamn, you're so sassy. I wanted to tame that mouth too." His thumb came up to replace his teeth. "Will you let me tame this pretty mouth?"

It took everything I had not to drop to my knees there, but somewhere in the back of my mind, our age difference lingered, and I wanted to be enough woman for him. I wanted to make him fight for it. We'd waited so long—danced around our want—that I wasn't going to be some easy teenager for him to fuck.

"Maybe. Will you let me tame yours?"

I shrieked when he growled, reaching down far enough to wrap his two large hands around my thighs and hoist me up around his waist. He made the decision for us and moved up the stairs, the wood creaking under our weight. Unable to help myself, I used my legs to rub up and down his abdomen, craving friction any way I could get it.

"Soaking through my fucking shirt."

"I need you," I whispered in his ear, growing desperate.

As quick as he picked me up, he stopped and set me down. We'd only made it halfway up the stairs, but he apparently needed me too.

He stood tall, looming above me, and whipped his shirt over his head, exposing every inch of rippling muscle. I swear I almost drooled.

Damn. Uncle Willem was hot.

No. Just Will tonight.

I didn't get much time to admire his body because he dropped to his knees a couple steps below and wedged his shoulders between my thighs, pushing my skirt up as he went. I opened my mouth to tell him I needed to take my skirt off to get to what he wanted, but it died in my throat when the tip of his tongue probed through the fabric right where I ached the most.

"Even through the cotton, you taste like fucking heaven. Let's see how you taste on my tongue."

He slipped his fingers under the elastic, brushing the lips of my pussy, before pulling the fabric to the side and diving in. His tongue brushed from the bottom of my opening all the way to the top just to swirl around my clit. I cried out and thrust up, the pleasure unlike anything I'd ever felt before.

He latched on and sucked, flicking his tongue back and forth like it was a race to my orgasm. My head fell back against the steps and one hand moved to palm my breast, helping him reach the finish line. As if he sensed my movement, his hand shot up to grip my wrist, pulling it away. With one last swipe, he leaned back, and I wanted to whimper at the loss.

"*I* touch you."

"Then do it."

Will delivered a smirk that rivaled mine, distracting me so much, I missed his hands lifting to rip my top down. My breasts popped free, the cool air hardening my nipples to tight points.

"Fuck, yes. Just as perfect as I imagined."

"You i-imagined me?" I breathed, stuttering over the words when his tongue flicked the tip.

"Yes."

"Did you touch yourself?"

"Yes."

Everything went hazy when he scraped his beard across one nipple and moved to the next. He circled the other bud with his tongue, not quite hitting the tip, and I wanted to grip his hair and direct him where I wanted. How did we get from a rushed frenzy to a slow, languid pace?

"Did you think of the way my tits would bounce as you fucked me? Ow," I gasped at the sharp pinch against the bottom of my breast.

"Don't push me."

"Someone has to."

We glared at each other without any actual anger, as if in an equal standoff. At least we were equal. I should have known he would knock me back when his smirk reappeared, and he slowly went back to pressing kisses to my nipples, traveling up my neck.

"Tell me, Arabella," he demanded against my skin, his hands moving to the waist of my skirt. "Has anyone ever eaten this tight little pussy? Is that why you're so eager to get me back there?"

I stared up at the ceiling and clenched my jaw, refusing to admit anything. But I did lift my hips when he tugged my skirt down, dragging it off my legs agonizingly slow when all I wanted to do was kick it off.

The rough pads of his fingers trailed up my thighs and gently brushed against my folds, slipping just enough between to torture, but not to touch my clit.

"Tell me, and maybe I'll do it again."

"No," I gasped, almost pleading. "No one has gone down on me."

"Good girl. Now," he sat back and spread my legs as wide as they'd go, baring every inch of me. "I want you to watch me. I want you to watch the way my tongue pushes inside and tastes every inch of you. I want you to watch when I suck your smooth folds into my mouth. I want you to watch my fingers disappear inside your cunt and come back out coated in your cream. I want you to watch the way my tongue circles your ripe little clit until you're screaming in pleasure."

I couldn't answer past the lump of need threatening to choke me, so I nodded.

"Good."

It was the last thing he said before he did exactly that. He looked up from between my thighs to make sure I watched every part. Neither of us said another word as he ate me like a starving man. Only my whimpers echoed off the walls when he finished like he said, his fingers in my cunt, his mouth sucking on my clit while his other hand tugged painfully at my nipple.

Gripping the edge of the wooden stairs so hard, I was sure I'd crack them, I came. I dug my heels into the wood and pushed against his thrusting hand and rubbed against his face, chasing every last second of my orgasm.

He kissed down my thigh once I finally settled, pulling his fingers from me with an obscene wet noise.

"I want you to go to your room and bend over the bed."

"What?" I asked breathlessly.

"Don't ask questions, Arabella. Just do it."

I wanted to rebel, to push back, but my mind had nothing left. I couldn't think on my own. Especially when he stood tall and started unfastening his belt and then his jeans. It was a solid reminder that we weren't done yet.

He stepped over me and walked to his room. When he disappeared behind the door, I scrambled as fast as my weak legs could carry me and did as he ordered. I'd never obeyed someone so easily as I did then.

It shocked me, but not quite as much as the fact that I liked it.

I stripped the rest of my clothes and rested my arms on the bed, waiting less than fifteen seconds before he loomed in the doorway.

"Spread your legs wider. Let me see it all."

I did, and he rewarded me with a deep groan.

I tried to look over my shoulder as he approached, but only got a glimpse of his chest before he stood too close to see. But I could hear. I could hear the tear of the condom wrapper. I could hear his jeans hit the floor and knew he stood naked behind me.

I could feel. I could feel the heat of his body so close, but not close enough. I could feel the touch of his fingers on my ankles as he trailed them up my legs.

Another whimper slipped free when he pushed his face

between my legs and licked my oversensitive clit, through my opening and all the way up the crack of my ass.

"Oh, god. Are you going to fuck me?"

I didn't think I could wait another second. I couldn't handle any more teasing.

"Probably more than once," he admitted between kisses up my back. "Are you okay with that?"

"Yes. Please," I begged.

He slapped my ass, the sting pulling a sharp moan from me. "Good."

And with that, he shoved inside me, stealing any more words I could form. He wasn't nice. He wasn't gentle and slow in discovery like other guys. He also wasn't quick, racing to his own orgasm without any concern for mine.

No. He alternated between quick, shallow thrusts and hard, bruising fucking. He'd hold my shoulders and push in as far and hard as he could go, pulling a wordless cry from my lips. When sweat slicked both our skins, he dug his hand in my hair and yanked me upright.

"Look," he ordered against my cheek.

I opened my eyes and looked at the mirror, finding my pale breasts bouncing in the moonlight. His tan skin wrapped around mine as he buried his hand between my thighs. His dark hair mashed against the wild mess of my red mane. We were flushed with the same desperate look.

"Fucking beautiful. With your tight little pussy milking my cock. Fuck, I'm gonna come."

"Yes. Yes."

"You first." He took two fingers and slapped my clit at the same time as pushing deep, and I came. I held on to his hips and fell apart, lost in the vision of us together.

His groan penetrated my haze, and I squeezed my core tighter, focusing on prolonging the orgasm for both of us.

His hand finally relaxed in my hair, and we fell over, where he quickly rolled his heavy weight off and slipped out.

"Jesus fucking Christ."

"Yeah," I agreed, gasping for air. "I'm gonna need a repeat performance as promised."

"Noted," he huffed. "Just give me a minute."

"Just a little while," I promised.

TEN

Willem

I MADE it to the classroom just in time. After showing up twenty minutes later than I planned, I also forgot my connecter cable for my laptop and had to run back to my office. The first day of classes was not the day to be distracted, and yet, there I was. My mind more focused on the most amazing sex I'd had over the last couple of nights rather than my job.

Hell, standing there in front of the room, pulling up the list of names in my class, my mind was still more focused on the image of Arabella bouncing on my cock this morning. On top of all that, I was on my third cup of coffee.

Because I was up all night and into the next day fucking Arabella—my niece, my stepbrother's daughter, a teenager fourteen years younger than me.

No matter how many ways I put it, I couldn't deny that I'd fucked up royally. But I also couldn't stop. I didn't want to. I'd even tried. Last night, I'd cornered her in the kitchen after dinner, and then again on the couch, trying to get her out of my system in an attempt to get a good night's sleep. It'd been a joke because before dawn, I'd still woken up in her bed after coming to her in the middle of the night for more.

More, more, more.

But it wasn't just her body I kept going back for. It was the moments between, when she curled in my arms, and we discussed the pros and cons of ways to travel. It was the conversations and debates and jokes and laughter that had got us there in the first place. It'd never been just about sex with her.

The sex had been a culmination of it all. She'd dug her way into my mind long before I craved her body. And the explosion of the last couple days made it impossible to ignore the way my heart thudded a little harder at just the thought of being with her. Before it'd been the hugs—the connection. It'd been the excitement of spending the evening with someone who got you —who saw you for you. I'd put it down to too many years alone.

But when I'd pushed open her door just after we'd said goodnight, the feeling returned, and it hadn't left until I did.

So, I stayed as long as I could, laughing with her long after I came, shoving past the truth that the weekend held more than just sex.

It left me tired and satisfied. But also distracted.

That's the only reason I could come up with how I completely missed her sitting in the first row of my class. Not even noticing until I stumbled over her name.

"Here," she answered.

My head snapped up. A white band T-shirt, black shorts that showed off her creamy thighs that I knew exactly how it felt to be between, and that sassy smirk.

After a hesitation that stretched on alarmingly long in my mind, I jerked back to attention, moving on to the next name.

What the hell was she doing in my class? She wanted to be a teacher. Had we talked about this? Had she mentioned it and I missed it?

If I'd been distracted before, it was nothing compared to having her warm brown eyes devouring me the entire class. I stumbled more than once over the syllabus and cut the class short when the questions running rampant in my brain became too much.

Just for a Little While

"Miss Colins. A word, please," I asked when only a few students still lingered in the room. Thankfully, they were too consumed by their own world to notice mine.

"Sure. In your office?"

I didn't miss the way she said office, and my mind flashed to her sitting on my desk, jokingly asking if she could earn her A another way.

With each step up the flight of stairs and down the hall, I took deep breaths, doing my best to ignore her behind me. Old students waved and colleagues said hi. I needed to be the beacon of professionalism despite that almost my entire focus was on keeping my erection under control.

As soon as the door closed, I asked, "What are you doing?"

She took her time, looking around my office again, cocking a brow when I made it a point to sit in my chair, hoping a desk between us would help. However, instead of sitting in the chair for students, she dragged her fingers along the desk, making her way to my side.

"Taking a class. Setting myself up for a better future, according to my parents," she teased.

"That's not what I meant. What are you doing in my class?"

"I thought it would be fun to take economics. It can't hurt to have a well-rounded education."

"Arabella…"

"Uncle Will," she said, laughter in her taunting voice.

"Jesus Christ. Please stop calling me that." She leaned against the edge of my desk, her long legs stretched out beside my chair, and I was useless to stop myself from taking in every inch, clenching the sides to keep from stroking her tempting flesh. Sitting tall, looking at papers on my desk, I tried for some semblance of control. "We're already walking a fine line, Arabella. Adding a student-teacher relationship on top of everything else is unprofessional. It's—"

"Hot."

Her interjection pulled my attention back to her. Not that it was hard.

God, that smirk. I'd yet to watch those lips wrap around me. I'd been too busy between her thighs. She tasted like heaven and knowing I'd been the only man to eat her pussy, only made me want to do it more.

"It's okay to admit. I know you're all professional and serious," she said with a scowl for effect before shifting back to a taunting smirk, her elegant fingers stroking her collar bone. "But you can admit it to me. I won't judge you. I can make your darkest fantasies come true."

"You couldn't handle my *darkest* fantasies."

"Try me."

"I can't do them here." Part of me wanted to try. Part of me wanted to whip off my belt and paint her ass red before fucking her against my desk. But we already toed the edge of getting caught. Her delicious cries of pleasure and pain would be too loud for the school day.

"Then we'll do those at home. But you can't say you've never fantasized about using your authority—your power—to gain pleasure."

Not exactly. Not outside of a consensual fantasy. I'd never once looked at a student in my class and thought about abusing my status. That didn't mean I hadn't fantasized about a faceless woman pleasuring her teacher.

My dick hardened, doing its best to escape my slacks and get to her.

I lost the battle when she brought both hands up and stroked them past the hard buds of her nipples poking against her shirt. I needed to have a conversation about her wearing a bra. Only because I didn't want others to see what was mine.

Mine?

I jerked away from the alarming thought—out of the frying pan and into the fire.

I dove headfirst into the forbidden—the illicit. The control.

"Get on your knees."

Her eyes blazed, widening like a kid in a candy shop. Without hesitation, she whipped off her shirt, exposing the creamy, pale breasts I'd grown to love, and fell to her knees. She rested her hands on my legs, inching her way between my thighs.

"Sit back. If anyone comes in, I don't want them to know I've got my fat cock down my student's throat."

"Yes, Dr. Deander."

So fucking wrong, and yet, as she adjusted, I unfastened my pants and pulled my hard length free, painting her lips with the leaking precum. Her tongue chased the head, tasting me.

"Now, take that sassy mouth of yours, wrap it around my cock, and make me come."

Her soft hand gripped my shaft and squeezed at the same time as her tongue flicked out to slip between the slit. I clenched my jaw, keeping my moan under control.

I almost lost it when everything I wanted became a reality, and her perfect, arrogant mouth wrapped around my dick and slid down, pulling back up, leaving a wet sheen behind.

Was there anything sexier?

I buried my hand in her hair and watched her bounce up and down, stopping every once in a while at the top to roll her tongue around the tip and suck on it like a popsicle. Each time she dropped, she'd go a little lower, pushing me past the soft barrier of her throat.

"One of these days, I'm going to lay you across my desk with your head hanging off, and I'm going to fuck your face. I'm going to watch my fat cock bulge against your throat over and over again until you swallow every fucking drop."

She couldn't respond with her mouth so full, but her answering moan let me know she liked it. The way she spread her thighs and rubbed at herself through her jean shorts let me know she was just as turned on as me.

I palmed her soft breast, pinched her pale, pink nipple until it was a rosy red. My scalp tingled and fire raced through every nerve of my body, electricity shooting down my spine. I was going to come.

"Is Dr. Deander in?" someone asked from behind the door. *Right behind.*

As fast as I could, I shoved Arabella off and sat up straight.

Adrenaline flooded my body so hard, I was sure I'd pass out. If I thought my skin had tingled before, it was nothing compared to the shock of fear—like I'd touched a live wire.

With Arabella still under my desk, sweat dampening my temples, my cock still out and hard, Dr. Coven walked in.

Would she leave if I threw up all over my desk? Because my stomach roiled as if I might. The only saving grace was that my desk had a back so no one could see under it.

"Dr. Coven," I managed in a mostly normal voice. "What can I do for you?"

"Oh, nothing. I just wanted to pop in and make sure you had everything you needed."

"Yeah. Everything is good."

"Are you okay? You look a little flushed. I know it's the first day, but no need to come in sick."

"Yeah, no. It's just a hot one out there. Killer walking between classes."

"Right? I'm hoping summer passes soon. It's not usually hot for so long."

I opened my mouth to respond with some benign answer when I almost choked on my own tongue.

A soft hand encircled my shaft just before warm lips dropped down. My erection had softened at the interruption, so Arabella was able to take me all the way to the base. Feeling her lips and nose press to my groin had me hardening again before she could pull back off, pressing into her throat.

Her throat closed, rejecting the intrusion, tightening around the head, and I held my breath waiting for her gagging to give her away, but she managed to not make a sound.

Dr. Coven asked about how my classes had been so far, if I had any issues with room placements or students. Somehow, I managed responses in a normal voice even though the more Arabella sucked, the more my world closed down to a pinprick. Being as discreet as possible, I reached under the table to stop her, fisting her hair. Instead of taking the silent reprimand, she dropped down again as far as my hold would allow.

Fuck. I was going to come and there was no way I could hide it. I clung to my composure with chipping nails against a knifes edge. One more push and it'd all be over.

"Well, I'll let you get back to it. I know the first day is hectic and wanted to check in. Let me know if you need anything."

"Will do."

The second the door closed behind her, I scooted back enough to grip Arabella's face and fucked my cock up into her mouth, coming within seconds. She did her best to swallow it all, but the way I kept slipping my dick in and out made a mess, and cum dripped down her chin to her breasts.

When I finally finished, I collapsed back in my chair, taking just a moment to breathe. My chest heaved over the pleasure of coming and the fear of being caught.

She leaned back and wiped her chin and breasts clean with her finger, bringing the extra cum to her lips to suck it off.

She was the epitome of no regrets.

She was a girl who had nothing to lose and only cared about the moment.

She was sexy.

And reckless.

The euphoria faded, and reality came crashing in. Looking away from her crouched on the floor, her breasts begging me to forget it all and continue our game, I handed her her shirt before fastening my pants.

I didn't trust what I'd say and needed a moment to collect myself. I also didn't trust myself to sit so close to her. Her red hair hung against her shoulders. She looked like a Siren begging for more. And I was a weak man who wanted to give it to her.

I shoved away from the desk and stood, pacing back and forth, rubbing a hand through my hair. When I turned, she thankfully had her shirt back on, but looked more unsure of herself than I'd ever seen.

"Will..." she started, opening the gates.

"What the hell do you think you're doing?"

"Umm...giving you a blow job?"

"Fuck, Arabella," I ground out, more frustrated with myself than her. I took her in, standing there with her shoulders pulled back, but doubt clouding her eyes despite trying to shove it behind her usual bravado. And I hated it. We'd bonded over our ability to just be, and here she was trying to put the veneer in place.

I hated it because I knew my frustration caused it.

I hated it because I knew before she left this office, it would get worse before it got better.

"This was a mistake." The words fell like dead weight, somehow making me lighter for saying the truth, but also crumbling under the weight of it.

"Okay. Sorry. I won't suck your cock at school again. Noted. I'll make sure to keep it at home."

"No, Arabella. All of it. Everything. Us. It's a mistake."

"What?" The veneer slipped, and her honest hurt knocked the wind out of me. Watching her, I saw every year between us. I saw the not yet twenty-year-old with a maturity unlike any other, but with so much left to learn. And just as quick as the veneer slipped, it went right back on. The arrogant girl who showed up on my steps three weeks ago back in place. "What do you mean mistake?" she asked, a hard edge in her voice. "Was it a mistake when you fucked me again and again. Did you slip and fall five times over the last two days into my open vagina? Was it a mistake when even after almost getting caught, you came in my mouth? Was it an accident?" she snapped, sarcasm pouring from the lips I already missed.

"You know it wasn't. This isn't easy, okay?"

"Seems like it."

Her inability to see reason broke my calm and my irritation snapped. "You know what? It fucking isn't. It isn't easy being the adult here, Arabella. It isn't easy to not be the teenager who doesn't give a fuck. You don't care if you get caught. Hell, you're probably hoping for it so you can get kicked out—which you wouldn't. You'd simply get removed from my class. But you know who would get kicked out? Me. This is my job. A career I've busted my ass for."

"You didn't seem to care too much when you ordered me to my knees and told me about how you'd fuck my throat. You didn't seem to care when I was swallowing your cum. You could have shoved me away, found a way to say stop. I didn't push you into it."

"I'm not saying you did."

"It sure feels like you're putting the blame on me."

"I'm not. *I'm* taking the blame. *I'm* the one that should know better. *I'm* the one who should have stopped it. I'm asking you to understand why this needs to stop. All of it. I respect your father. Jesus," I laughed. "I'm your fucking uncle."

"You are *not* my uncle."

"It's still too close. I'm the adult here, and I messed up."

"I'm not some kid."

"I know that. Trust me, I *know* that. I wish I could see you that way. It would make my life a lot easier if I didn't find you so damn irresistible. If I didn't find myself wanting you—and not just your body."

"So, if we're both adults, what's wrong?"

"What's wrong is you're too young and arrogant and stubborn to not see what's wrong with it. You're too young to make the right decision."

As soon as the words left my mouth, I knew they'd be the

final blow. They hit too close to what her parents said to her. They hit too close to her worst insecurities.

"Fine." This time when she pulled on a mask, it held nothing. No anger, no irritation, no hurt, no nothing. "I have another class to get to."

"Arabella, wait. We need to talk."

"No. We don't. You've made it quite simple. Thank you."

And before I could say anything else, she left, leaving me with regrets that would last longer than the little while that got us here.

ELEVEN

Arabella

THE LAST TWO weeks were a complete one-eighty from our relationship before sleeping together. Pre-sex: hugs, hand holding, watching tv, shared dinners, lunches and breakfasts, story time on the couch with my head on his shoulder. Post sex: none of that. The only consistency was the ever-growing tension that pulled tighter and tighter between us.

But that mostly existed because I pushed for it. Maybe it was the arrogance he callously threw at me. Maybe it was my pride. Maybe it was the hope that he would figure out how much I missed him, and he'd admit he missed me too, and we could move past it.

I wiped away the steam from the bathroom mirror, trying to shove down the self-recrimination I saw every time I looked at myself. As much as I hated everything he said and as mad as it made me, he wasn't wrong. I could see what was wrong with what we'd done. But I also cared enough about my feelings to weigh the pros and cons and know he was worth it.

I knew I shouldn't have started the game in his office. I definitely should have stopped when we almost got caught. But I hadn't, and I was paying the price.

However, he lashed out with his words and denials. So, I made him pay the price every day.

His footsteps came closer down the hall, and I flung the bathroom door open, the pleasure of winning bringing my skin to life when he almost stumbled to a stop and took me in wearing a too-small white towel precariously wrapped around me.

"Uncle Will?"

"Jesus," he sighed to himself.

Yeah, I was making it worse, but I wanted him to admit this wasn't all a mistake. I wanted him to take back his words about being immature and belittling me. I wanted him to regret hurting my feelings.

"Can I have friends over this weekend? We wanted to swim in the pool before it got too cold."

"You couldn't have asked me in the car?"

And miss his eyes trying and failing to not take me in? I shrugged. "I was thinking about it now."

"Yeah," he sighed in defeat. "How many people?"

"Just three or four."

"Fine."

With that, he moved to leave, and just before I closed the door, I dropped the towel, smiling over his muttered *fuck me.*

After that show, I gave him a small reprieve in the car and kept silent. Besides, we had class later, and I had plans.

He always tensed up when I walked into the room. This time even more since I sat in the very front when I usually sat in the middle. His eyes kept flicking to me, probably wondering why I moved seats.

At about fifteen minutes into his lecture, I removed my jacket, my nipples growing hard when he faltered over his words and stared. He recovered quickly enough so no one noticed, but I had. I knew he saw the way the thin white shirt barely covered my nipples. The material so thin and tight you could see the pale areola and hard tips.

Just for a Little While

Whenever his attention snagged on me, I'd brush my fingers subtly across my chest, making it hard to sit still in my seat. Each stroke across my nipples sent a shock to my core, and thirty minutes in, I ached.

It wasn't until the end that my plan faltered. I'd been so focused on teasing him that I'd stopped paying attention to what he actually said.

"Miss Colins?"

"Umm...yeah?"

"Yeah, isn't the answer."

The class's attention focused on me, and I sat forward, hiding what I'd flaunted for him. Heat flooded my cheeks with each whisper in the seconds that ticked by in my silence. "I didn't hear the question. Could you repeat it?" I asked, striving for a confidence I didn't feel.

His jaw clenched under his scruff. "I asked if anyone could explain price elasticity of demand."

Shit. I vaguely remembered reading it but couldn't recall off the top of my head. "Uh, yeah. Let me look it up," I said, flipping the pages of my book.

"Can someone who actually read tell me?" he asked the class, dismissing my attempt.

Hands shot up, and I sank back in my seat, thoroughly embarrassed, struggling through the last five minutes of class. When he dismissed us, I shoved everything in my bag, my head down, desperate to regroup. Just as I stood, his voice stopped me from escape.

"A word, Miss Colins."

"Good luck," a guy I sat next to whispered.

I managed an annoyed smile with an eye roll, acting like being called after class was no big deal.

Once the class cleared out, Will moved in front of the desk and leaned back, crossing his arms and legs.

"Do you even like this class? Or are you just wasting time and money so you can torture me?"

"It was one question, Will."

"In the first month of class. A question you should have been able to answer. It only gets harder from here."

"I was distracted."

"Yeah, I noticed."

"Oh, don't act like you weren't distracted." I wanted to provoke him into admitting he couldn't take his eyes off me because he wanted me.

"The difference was, that I didn't want to be. You want to drop your towel at home? Fine. But keep it there, Arabella. This is my job, and this is your education. Stop being so selfish and really think about what you're doing. Is this *really* what you want to do?"

"I'm not a child," I defended. Like a child.

I didn't know how to answer, and it scared me sober, leaving me to lash out.

He shook his head, rolling his eyes at my snotty remark, refusing to feed into it. This time, no one had to look at me with disappointment—I was disappointed in myself.

"I'm not saying you are. I'm asking you a very mature question. You've been so pissed about being forced to be here and pissed over your parents not accepting who you want to be, but have you ever stopped to think about what you *do* want?"

The situation slipped from my hands. I'd barely held on to it after he called on me, but sitting in a desk with him looming over, asking me questions I didn't know the answer to left me at a loss. Everything closed in, and all the unimportant things like torturing Will fell away.

One question rattled around, shaking everything else free.

What do you want?

"I—I don't know. I guess no one has asked me," I admitted, coming to the realization even as I said the words.

"*I'm* asking now."

In that moment, I wanted to stand up and hug him. I wanted to find the old comfort and understanding in his arms like I had before. In that moment, I realized what I'd really been fighting for. It hadn't been for him to admit he wanted me. He'd already said that. I wanted him to come to me and tell me he missed me. Missed watching tv. Missed coming home to my embrace. Missed laughing with me. Missed just *me*. Something no one had ever missed before.

In that moment, I let it all go and dropped all pretenses, giving him my honest self like I had before. "I want to travel."

"I do too, but you can't just wander around forever aimlessly. Trust me, I tried. You need a plan. If that includes economics, then great. If not, then stop wasting everyone's time and go talk to your counselor to figure out what your plan does include. Just…stop being so angry and do something about it."

After his speech, I didn't have anything left to say. He'd said it all and took the wind out of my sails while he said it. Feeling embarrassed by my actions that brought us here, ashamed of acting like the child I constantly demanded he stop treating me like, I kept quiet. Instead, opting to nod my head, letting him know I heard him, and standing to go.

He gave me a nod of his own. Enough words had been said today, and I think we were both too tired to argue anymore.

My chest ached with each step toward the door. His honesty hurt, but I'd appreciated he'd said it. In his own way, it had been him admitting he cared, and that eased the pain.

"Willem?" I called from the door.

He looked up from where he packed his bag. "Yeah?"

"Thank you."

"Any time. And not just for a little while. Any time you need me—*really* need me—I'm here."

TWELVE

Willem

WORKING on a Saturday wasn't exactly my top pick on how to spend my weekend, but after the collision after class earlier this week, we'd been avoiding each other. I made sure she knew I could pick her up from work, drive her anywhere she needed to go, or take my car if it was free. But as classes went on, she made friends, and they gave her rides. Hell, as much as she'd been working, she'd be able to buy a car in no time.

I didn't blame her for avoiding me. Tuesday had been a mess. Hell, all of this was a mess, but my hot spot was work, and she knew it. I'd worked too damn hard to get here to fuck it up. She talked about wanting to make her plans around traveling. Well, economics had been my ticket to travel. It'd been my plan.

Nowhere in that plan included a fiery, stubborn, young woman who challenged me every step of the way.

But I couldn't stop wondering if maybe it should.

I missed her.

I kind of even missed the way she tortured me at home.

I definitely missed the hugs.

I missed her body. I'd only had it for a few days, but it'd been enough to become ingrained in my identity.

More than her body, I missed her mind—her soul. I missed

our talks. The debates and plans for places we still wanted to see.

She'd found a hole I hadn't known was there and burrowed herself inside me. Before her, it'd been irrelevant, and now, it yawned like a gaping bullet wound I ached for her to wrap her arms around and make better.

She had so much to give—so much to still do. No one had just let her go for it with their full support. She did all her actions and created all her success in defiance. More of a fuck you to everyone she wanted to prove wrong rather than actually making decisions about what she wanted her future to be. I hated how it all played out but remembering her soft thank you at the end was the silver lining.

Laughter echoed through the screen door out back, pulling me from the depressing thoughts that I couldn't chase away. I dropped my bag at the steps and walked down the hall to make sure all was well. I didn't speed up just to see her. It was to make sure a rave wasn't destroying my barely used backyard.

Not ready to announce my presence, I stood back a bit from the window and almost swallowed my tongue.

The two blondes from her work splashed around in the pool, and another girl and guy I didn't know sat on the edge talking to Arabella and *fucking* Xander. Arabella hunched over, gripping the ledge, looking to be about two seconds away from her breasts spilling out of the tiny scraps of fabric. The top was more string than anything else. The black triangles stood out, stark against her pale skin, making the material look even smaller.

Fuck me. If I'd stumbled upon her like this pre-battle, I'd assume she wore that bathing suit to torture me more. But she'd stopped the past few days, and I knew she wore that suit for her. I refused to think she wore it for Xander.

Her smirk firmly in place, I knew the Instagram version of Arabella sat out there, and I hated it. I hated the way every man, including me, stopped to stare at her breasts swaying when she reached an arm up to brush her hair back. I hated the way Xander bumped his shoulder to hers and leaned in to say something close to her ear.

I hated how fake I knew it was. I hated it all.

Grabbing a beer, I cracked it open and made my way out.

"Dr. Deander," one of the blonde's shouted. "Are you coming to swim, too?"

"As much as I appreciate the offer, I'll leave the pool to you guys."

"Boo," she pouted. "I was hoping to have a partner to play chicken with."

"Sorry to let you down. Maybe next time."

The false offer settled her enough to give her attention back to the other blonde, leaving me to shift my attention to Arabella.

For one moment, I saw the girl from before. I saw the clenched jaw. I saw the spark of obstinance like she wanted to do something to lay claim to me in front of her coworker, but just as quick, she shut it down, giving me the same neutral smile she gave everyone else at the pool.

"Thanks for letting us use your pool, Dr. Deander," Xander said.

"Of course."

Xander poked Arabella in the ribs, making a joke about being her partner in chicken, his eyes glued to her swaying breasts. It took all I had to not call him on it and demanded she put on a shirt.

I hated that she flirted back. I hated that she didn't taunt me. Unlike the mature adult I claimed to be, jealousy sparked. I wanted her to show me she wanted me because, despite it being wrong, I couldn't stop wanting her.

We'd connected on a level I hadn't seen coming and watching her flirt with someone else was too much.

With a muttered offer to let me know if they needed anything, I went inside, grabbing another beer on my way. Once I changed, I headed to my office, the one room without any windows looking into the backyard and shut the door to block out any sound.

I pulled up emails, watched a show on Netflix, googled tickets to fly to a remote island and forget the last couple of months. None of it helped, and after only a couple hours, I found myself making my way downstairs again. I promised I'd run down to grab a beer and head back up.

All that went to shit when I rounded the corner to the kitchen and found her standing in front of the sink, her back to me, the bottom of her bikini just as revealing as the top. The firm globes of her ass almost completely bare, firm like a ripe peach I wanted to fall to my knees and sink my teeth into. So pale I wanted to have her bend over, brace her hands on the counter, and spank her for each time I'd had to jack off over the last few weeks, just so I could watch the red bloom beautifully against her skin.

As if my body had enough of my mind holding back, it moved without thought to her, like a moth to a flame. She was so focused on what she was doing she didn't notice my approach until I caged her in, my hands resting on the counter on either side of her, my body inches from pressing into hers.

She gasped and looked to the side, her soft hair brushing across my face. Leaning in closer until my lips almost touched her ear, I asked, "Where's your boy toy?"

"What?" she asked, her voice low and rough, letting me know she was just as affected as me.

"Xander."

"Are you jealous?" she snipped.

I ran my nose against the soft skin of her cheek, wanting to drown in the scent of coconut and her. "You know I am."

She forced her way around, leaning back to stare up into my eyes. Unable to help it, my gaze dropped down her body, groaning at the close up of her breasts. I grew harder, taking in the soft indents on her hips, remembering how I held her there as I fucked her from behind. Her nipples hardened under the thin material of her top as I took her in, and I clenched the counter to stop from pulling her bottoms aside to find out if her pussy missed me as much as her nipples did.

Coasting up her neck, past her parted lips, I finally met her eyes, finding them soft and wanting. I wanted to drown in them, give her everything and more. The need bloomed from my chest, down my arms, urging me to just do it. A flicker of movement from the window pulled my attention to Xander, reigniting my jealousy.

"Willem." She said my name softly like a plea.

The warmth filling me ignited with a tinge of fire from watching Xander touch her earlier.

"Will you let him fuck you?"

She blinked, her eyes widening. "Wha—"

"Will you let him slip your panties aside and touch you? Will you let him be the second man to taste your pretty little pussy?" I leaned in closer, crowding her back. Her hands landed on my chest, and I brushed my lips past her cheek without kissing anything. "Will you come for him like you did me? Hold him where you want him and ride his face?"

Her nails dug in, making us both groan. "Please, Willem."

Unable to stand it anymore, I caved and found her mouth with mine. She met me halfway, the kiss hard and desperate. Our lips mashed without finesse, our tongues dueling for dominance, tasting each other like we may never get to again. She pushed off the counter, pressing against my hard cock, her soft breasts against my chest.

Needing to feel them, I finally let go of the counter and filled my hands with her body. I kissed down her neck and tugged the fabric aside, baring her pale nipple.

"Fuck," I muttered.

She thrust herself up toward my mouth and ground against my groin.

The flash of Xander watching her earlier had me wanting to lay claim—to mark her as mine. I bit and sucked at her nipple, torturing the tip with my mouth as my hand played with the other before moving my lips just under the nipple where it couldn't be seen in the bathing suit, but impossible to ignore without it.

Without any regrets, I sucked and sucked, leaving my mark. Pleased with my work, I moved to the other side and repeated the process. By the time I'd finished, she had one leg over my hip, her wet pussy soaking through her suit, and my jeans.

I was ready to lift her to the counter and fuck her right there with her guests outside the window. Hell, I didn't care if they came in. They could watch me make her mine. They could watch her fall apart for me like she did with no one else.

"Bella," one of the girls called from outside, like a bucket of cold water over the moment. As if that wasn't bad enough, they pretty much handed us a live wire and doused us again, shocking us back to reality with their next words. "Your dad is calling."

Her dad.

My stepbrother, who I admired. Who helped me when I struggled. Who'd never forgive what I was doing to his daughter if he found out.

"Shit," I whispered.

With that reminder, I tugged the tiny triangles back over her breasts and stepped back, unable to meet her eyes.

"Will," she almost pleaded.

"Your friends are waiting."

"Will, please, don't."

How could I not? Just because my caveman needs outweighed my ability to make a decision about right and wrong didn't change our situation. Even if I was her teacher. Even if I was too old for her. Even if we could move past that. How did we move past her family? *My* only family?

I needed to get back under control and let her be with someone less complicated. Even if it hurt.

I turned to walk out, but stopped before leaving the kitchen, issuing one rule to save my sanity. "Just no sex in the house."

And like the mature adult I was, I ran, promising to stay in my room the rest of the night. And unlike all the other promises we'd made, I intended to keep this one. For both our sakes.

THIRTEEN

Arabella

Son-of-a-mother-fucking-bitch.

If I'd ever wanted to cuss out my dad before, it didn't come close compared to now. Finally, after weeks of wanting and fighting and then deciding to sit back to stop chasing, everything I wanted happened. Willem was kissing me. Willem was touching me. Willem was back in my arms, making it right again.

Only to pull back one more time, demanding not to fuck in the house. Like he didn't even care if I slept with Xander. It pissed me off. His hot and cold and back to hot was like oxygen to a fire. After our argument, I'd promised to step back, to stop torturing him, and let it be. I'd hoped that we'd find our norm again and it would work out. The connection we'd formed so quickly couldn't be denied for long, and I'd pushed for it with sex, but the reality was that we hadn't gotten there with sex. We'd gotten there by listening to each other, by spending time and falling for each other.

The sex had been the culmination of all that, and I'd wanted to recreate that bond no matter how much time it took.

That had been the plan until he'd come into the kitchen, reigniting the fire in me. He'd doused the waiting embers in gasoline, and between the need and frustration and want, I was ready to explode.

The stubborn, petulant side of me considered defying him and taking Xander to my room. It'd serve him right to know Xander would be the one to pleasure me—to see my naked body. He'd be the one sucking on my brea—

"No," I breathed.

A thought slammed in my head, stopping my revenge plot like a scratched record. The fantasy of Xander being the one to stare at my breasts had me wondering what he would see. The spot where Willem's mouth clung moments ago tingled.

"No. He wouldn't." I ran down the hall to the bathroom and closed the door, tugging my top aside, and sure enough, two hickeys decorated the underside of my breasts, like stark beacons laying claim to me so no one else could.

"That mother fucker."

I almost ran straight upstairs, ready for battle. But the laughter from out back reminded me of my guests—guests I needed to leave because there was no way I could shove anything down for later.

A hurricane of emotions whirled inside me, growing bigger with each step to the backyard, so when I finally made it out, all semblance of politeness was gone.

"Everyone needs to leave."

Five confused faces turned my way, but I didn't care. I needed them gone because I needed privacy for the explosion that lingered on the horizon.

"Please," I added, trying to soften the amount of crazy pouring off me. "Something came up."

It took less than five minutes for everyone to pile out. Five minutes too long where I rudely cut off any questions or comments, too focused on what was to come.

Willem Deander had cared for me, fucked me, shut me down, and made me feel immature. He'd ignored me and embarrassed me—when I deserved it—and lit a fire in me again just to shut it down—again. He'd told me not to fuck anyone in his house, knowing damn well I couldn't because he'd marked me anyway.

My independence raged at being controlled with his backhanded actions. My body burned from what he'd done, remembering his mouth on me. My heart thudded harder than before because he cared, but I was terrified it wasn't enough.

Like all other times in my life, stubbornness and arrogance won out. So, once everyone cleared the driveway, I stomped up the stairs right to his room and flung the door open, storming in.

"What the hell do you think you're doing?"

He jerked up, eyes wide, setting his book aside. "What?"

"What? You don't want me, but no one else can have me?"

"Arabella," he sighed my name and stood from the chair by the window.

"Don't Arabella me. You fucking marked me and then left me. What if I wanted to fuck Xander tonight? What if I *did* want him to eat my pussy so I could ride his face." His fists clenched, and victory sparked, knowing I was getting to him. I'd backed off and look where that got us. I was tired of running. We were facing this. "Maybe I wanted to sit on his cock as he sucked my tits. Maybe I wanted to see if it felt as good when he bit them as when you did."

"Stop," he growled, taking two challenging steps closer.

"Why? Why fucking should I?"

"Because us together is wrong. I'm older than you. I'm your uncle."

"Oh, here we go," I said, rolling my eyes. "I don't know why you're so adamant about clinging to this stupid thought that I'm actually your niece." When he didn't answer, I pushed harder, needing a reaction, knowing it was a weak excuse and wanting him to finally admit it. "Is it because secretly you like it? Does it turn you on thinking of me as your niece? Another forbidden fantasy?"

His warning glare only spurred me on, and he knew it, my

smirk a warning for what was to come. We both knew he didn't want this scene, but I'd be damned if I was the first one to cave. I went to the bed, undoing my bikini top, letting it fall to the floor on the way.

"Stop," he almost pleaded.

Instead, I rested my hands against the mattress and pushed my ass out. "Come on, Uncle Willem. Come fuck your little niece."

"Don't call me that," he growled.

Giving him my best pout, I spread my legs wider. "I've been a bad girl, Uncle Willem. Will you spank me?"

Two more steps and he closed the distance between us, digging his hand in my hair and pulling me up against him, so he could issue his order in my ear. "Stop calling me that."

Oh no. I wasn't done yet.

I slid my hands up my stomach to my breasts, fingering my nipples, feeling his moan vibrate against my back. "Please, Uncle Willem. Make my little girl pussy feel better. Fill your niece's tiny cunt with your big fat cock."

His head dropped into my neck and his hands came up to cover mine, halting their movement by slipping his fingers between mine, almost clinging to me. "Arabella. Please," he begged. "You know I don't want that. You know it's just a thin excuse to try and keep some distance. You know I want you— the woman."

The sincerity in his voice—the admission of the truth— finally broke through. The way he clung to me like a man on the edge of losing it had me extracting myself from his grip and turning in his arms, pulling him into my tightest embrace.

Just like before it all went to shit, his arms wrapped around me, holding me almost too tight.

But I didn't care. If he held me so tight, I took my last breath in his arms, then so be it.

And in that moment, I knew I loved him.

I loved the way he held me and made me feel safe. I loved

the way he accepted me and encouraged me to be better than before. I loved that he saw me and never asked for anything else.

Slowly, the hug softened, our hands that were digging into each other moments before, eased and began stroking, touching any inch we could reach.

"God, I've missed this," he breathed against my neck.

"I've missed you." He pulled back enough to stare down at me, indecision and hurt and want mixing like a hurricane unsure of which direction to go. Would he shove it down and send it back out to sea or let it break free and consume us both. I knew what I wanted, and I let him see every need and want in my eyes too. "Please, Will."

Please don't hurt me. Please don't pull away. Please don't stop. Please, please, please. I wanted to fall to my knees and beg him to do all the right things I wasn't sure how to ask for.

Like a storm I knew would happen, he crashed into me. His mouth slammed into mine, consuming me. His tongue pushed at my lips, and I opened, greedy for more. My body burned, flames spreading from where his fingers dug into my back to where my nipples scraped against his shirt, down to my core.

Feeling entirely too underdressed compared to him, I fumbled with his jeans, my fingers shaking from the flood of adrenaline as I ripped at the button and eased the zipper down. Not bothering to tease any more than I already had, I dropped to my knees and pulled his pants down.

"Arabel—"

My name choked off to a groan when I sucked the fat head of his cock between my lips, looking up at him the whole time. I slid down as far as I could go, moaning when he stripped off his shirt, baring each rippling muscle for my viewing pleasure. Unable to resist temptation, I slid my hand up, fingering each divot of his abs until I reached his nipple, pinching. He grunted and thrust, hitting the back of my throat.

One hand buried in my hair and the other shifted to repay

the favor, twisting and pulling at my breasts as he pushed me down over and over again on his cock.

Too soon, he pulled me off, and I whimpered my disappointment.

"I need to be inside you."

He helped me stand before tossing me on the bed. I bounced and scooted back, watching him strip his pants and stalk to the nightstand, almost ripping the drawer off in his eagerness to get a condom.

Watching him roll the condom over each inch had me on the brink of fingering myself right then and there, not even wanting to wait the ten seconds for him to get between my thighs.

As if he could read my mind, he placed a knee on the bed and glared. "Don't even think about it."

"I wasn't going to do anything."

"I know that look," he said with arrogance.

"What look is that?"

"The one that says you're on edge and too impatient to wait for anyone else, so you'll do it yourself. The one that says I want what I want, and you can't stop me." He crawled between my thighs, untying the strings at my hips painstakingly slow. "Is your pussy eager for me? Does it want my fingers?" he asked, stroking his fingers through my wet folds and circling my clit. "My mouth?" He brought his fingers to his lips and sucked my cream from them, closing his eyes and letting out a moan. "Or to be filled with my cock?" He rubbed the head of his shaft up and down my slit, pushing in the tiniest bit. "Hmm, Arabella? Which one do you need?"

"All of it, please. Just stop torturing me."

"I should tease you—drag this out for hours after the way you've tortured me the past few weeks."

"Willem, please."

"Lucky for you, I'm eager too. So, I'll pay you back later. Right now, I just need to be inside you."

With one slow thrust, he pushed all the way to the hilt, holding my eyes the whole time.

The air in my lungs slipped free, barely rushing back in before he did it again, stealing any oxygen again and again. As if he couldn't decide what he missed more, my hugs or my body, he fell over me, holding me tight, fucking me hard and fast and then harder and slow.

I clung to him just as tightly, kissing every inch I could reach, pressing my breasts to his chest, so each thrust caused them to bounce against his chest hair.

"So fucking tight. Like you were made for me."

Running my hand through his hair, I pulled him back to look at me.

"Maybe I was."

His brilliant blue eyes swirled between heat and so much caring and need I could only hope it was anywhere near the same love that filled me. I couldn't be the only one in this.

He ran his nose along mine, delivering the sweetest, softest kiss against my lips. "Maybe you were."

"Willem…" I wanted to say it then. I wanted to confess how much he meant to me as my eyes burned, the emotions too much.

Before the words could slip free, he sat up, pulling me with him. "Ride me."

Resting my forehead to his, I flexed my thighs and rocked back and forth. His hand moved to my ass, pushing to urge me faster, pulling a gasp from my parted lips when his finger slipped between the crack to brush against another place no one had ever touched.

"Oh, god."

"Someday," he promised.

It was the sweetest promise I'd ever heard because it wasn't some illicit promise to claim every inch of me. It was a promise that there would be a time in the future when we were still together.

It spurred me on, and I rocked harder.

"Good girl," he encouraged. "You fuck me so well. So hard, I'm going to come."

"Yes. Yes."

"Come for me," he ordered.

I rode harder, chasing the orgasm he demanded I have. "Help me," I begged. "Give me more." My plea fell with double meaning, and his hooded eyes let me know he understood both.

His hand slipped between my thighs and brushed against my clit, his other gripping my ass so tight I hoped for bruises in the morning. I held on to him, our bodies slick, my eyes glued to his, and with only a few swipes across my swollen bundle of nerves, I came.

My hands dug into his hair, and I held him to me, tears leaking from the corner of my eyes as my world exploded and pulsed and slammed back together, all in his arms. He circled my clit, easing me down from my orgasm, just to grip both my hips and raise up to his knees, holding me in place as he fucked me like a freight train.

My pussy pulsed with aftershocks on the verge of coming again when I looked down at his tight abs, straining arms, and thick, fat dick tunneling in and out of me.

When he reached his orgasm, he toppled us over, sliding as deep as he could, and I latched on to his lips wanting to taste his moan. I dragged my fingers through his hair, past his neck, and across his shoulders, just to reverse the path and do it all over again.

My thighs ached from having them spread around him, but I never wanted to move. I was uncertain what happened once he slipped free, and the immature girl inside me wanted to stay like this forever. I wanted to stomp my feet and cross my arms, refusing to move.

With as much hesitance as I felt, he slipped free, easing the separation with a long kiss. He softly drank from my lips. As frantic as they were before, they were languid and exploring now.

"Let me get rid of the condom," he whispered against my mouth. "Then we can sleep a bit before going again."

Before he could get up, I gripped his wrist, holding him in place. Not even being able to meet his eyes in fear I'd see the answer before he said it. I wanted to prolong any pain as long as possible, so I stared at where I gripped him and asked, "And tomorrow?"

The longest pause of my entire life followed.

My heart crumpled in on itself when he twisted his wrist out of my grasp. Tears burned up my nose as I struggled to swallow down the lump, fighting with all I had not to sob in his bed and beg him to not do this.

His finger stroked my chin, forcing it up so I looked at him, and I saw the last thing I expected.

A smirk to rival mine. Full of arrogance and an emotion I was too scared to hope for.

"Tomorrow, there's a special marathon on the best hidden cities in Russia and Europe. I figured we could order food, curl up on the couch, and pick our favorites."

Euphoria slammed into me. More than I ever thought possible.

One of my favorite experiences abroad was when I had woken up early in Scotland and climbed the highest mountain in the UK. I'd struggled and thought about going back at least a hundred times. But the happiness I felt at the top—feeling beyond lucky when the rain stopped, and the sun peeked out. It was like the clouds parted just for me.

That feeling had nothing on what Will's words did to me.

I thought I'd float off the bed. My heart, where moments ago tried to crumble in on itself, grew to almost bursting. Nothing could stop the smile that took over.

His thumb traced my lips, and he smiled like the skies parted just for him too. "I love it when you smile. It's so rare to get more than a smirk that it makes it all the more special."

Wrapping my lips around the tip, I kissed him and rubbed my cheek like a cat against his palm.

He went to stand again, and I gripped his wrist one more time, sitting up.

I couldn't hold it back anymore, and if for some reason he went into the bathroom and looked at himself in the mirror and saw a reason to come back with another answer, I needed to say it now.

He turned to me with furrowed brows, and I clung to him, terrified he'd pull back but more terrified he'd never know.

"I'm falling in love with you."

His smile slowly grew with hesitance.

"I know it comes with a million strings attached, but I don't care. Call me immature or selfish or childish. I don't care, Will. I'm falling for you, and I do know that I've never felt this before, and I don't want to hide it. And I know that love is hard and that if we want it enough, we can make it work."

"Fuck," he muttered, finally just stripping the condom and dropping it on the hardwood floor. "I'll clean it later." With that, he climbed back in bed and pulled me into his arms, holding me tight.

I climbed on his lap, wrapping around him. This was how we showed our love. This was how we showed how much we cared. By holding on tight and comforting in a way no one else ever had.

Even if he didn't say it back, I had this. He hadn't called a stop to everything at my proclamation, and I'd take it. As long as he didn't leave my side, we could grow from there—together.

He pulled back, pushing my hair back from my still damp forehead, his eyes bouncing all around my face like he didn't know where to look first. Finally, he settled on my eyes, stroking my cheek.

"I'm falling in love with you too."

This time when tears came, I let them fall, too happy to bother stopping them. He huffed a laugh and brushed them aside. "I've never said it to anyone, but I didn't expect you to cry at my proclamation," he teased.

"I'm just so happy, I don't know what to do with it."

"I have a few ideas."

He kissed me again, but only for a bit.

"We have to hide it at school. At least until the semester is over. No more teasing."

I rolled my eyes in jest. "Fine. But I guess I should let you know I dropped your class yesterday. I spoke to my counselor, and we both agreed economics wasn't in my plan. Even if the professor is."

His proud smile washed over me. "Good. Although you're missing out. Economics is the best."

Another eye roll had him laughing.

"Your dad..." he started.

"Will have to understand. He's important to both of us, and I know he's your family. But I'm your family now, too, and I promise to stand by you no matter what."

"I promise to stand by you too."

Any more happiness, and I was sure I'd burst like a balloon any second if I didn't give some of it to him. I rocked in his lap, kissing and biting along his jaw, my teeth scraping against his scruff.

He groaned, but gripped my ass, pulling me closer. "I need to eat and refuel."

"We will. I just want to kiss you. Just for a little while."

And just like when all this started, we made the promise, both of us knowing it was a lie.

We were so much more than just a little while.

Willem

EPILOGUE

4 Years Later

"Arabella Colins."

I watched proudly from my seat as she crossed the stage, her trademark smirk fully in place. She held it there, up until she shook hands with the school president, and shouts and applause broke out in small cells around the ceremony. Shouts from further away from her mom and dad, and high-pitched whistles and catcalls from her friends in the mix of students.

It took all I had not to join them.

She scanned the crown, her lips fighting the losing battle to remain pinched closed. When her eyes finally locked with mine, she lost, and the smile I'd fallen more in love with each day over the last four years shined through.

I love you, she mouthed.

My chest puffed up that this beautiful, brilliant woman loved me—chose me every day—even when it was hard.

We'd hit our ups and downs, especially when Harry found out about us—in the worst way possible. With my hand shoved down her bikini bottoms in their pool house the summer after her freshman year. We'd planned to tell him...just not like that.

My jaw still hurt from the punch he landed.

When he'd kicked me out, Arabella had followed and stood by my side every second of the three months he refused to talk to me, reminding me of her love at every doubt and turn.

We'd made it through every semester abroad she did.

We made it through the semester she decided to give the dorms a try.

We made it through every handsy guy I wanted to pummel at the bar. Thankfully, she finally quit yesterday.

We made it through the explaining of our relationship to the Dean of Economics when Arabella ended up having to take some economics courses.

We stood by each other as she grew into the woman I loved. I never wanted to hold her back from the growth she embraced with both arms. When we started all this, she was nineteen, determined and stubborn to make her way even if it meant barreling headfirst through cement.

At the end of the ceremony, the woman walking toward me learned that maybe using the door could get her to the other side with much less struggle and damage. Although, she tended to kick the door down each time, and I loved it.

"Dr. Deander," she greeted. "Or Uncle Will?" she asked in a breathy voice.

I scowled.

She laughed.

"Fine, Dr. Uncle Will."

"I swear to god," I grumbled. "What am I going to do with you?"

"I can think of quite a few things. Wanna find a closet and try them out?" She nodded her head to the side, biting into her plump lip and sliding her arms around my shoulders.

"I'm going to need more room than a closet for all I want to do with you," I promised.

She stepped indecently close, pressing her groin to mine.

Thank god for this oversized graduation robe to hide the effect she had on me.

"Will you keep the hat? It's so kinky."

I snorted, tugging the fluffy velvet cap off my head. Her long fingers dove into the messy strands and attempted to tame them, really only serving to turn me on more.

"Arabella," Arabella's mom greeted. She came toward us with her arms out, and Bella abandoned my arms for her mothers.

Not that I minded—much. I liked watching Arabella hug her mom. Another thing that'd come a long way over the years. Diana had come around a lot quicker than Harry, and I think Arabella just wanted an ally. In that time, they talked, bridging the gap of misunderstanding between them. Now, every time they were together, Arabella was treated to the mom-hugs that had started that conversation all those years ago.

Every now and then, Diana would treat me to one too—even if she was only a decade older, it's like a flip switched when you had a kid, and your hugs carried a whole new meaning. I loved it.

"Willem," Harry greeted much more stoically than his wife.

"Harry."

We nodded, not quite where we used to be, but getting there. When his silence carried on too long and began digging at Arabella, I took an overnight trip to Colorado and faced him. Letting him know how much I loved his daughter, and despite the numerous issues on paper, none of them mattered because this was forever.

I'd demanded he, at the very least, stop punishing Arabella.

Since then, we'd inched our way back to normal—it just took him a couple of hours to relax. Also, a few beers never hurt either.

"Look at you," Diana gushed, looking Arabella up and down.

"You just saw me and took pictures already."

"I know, but now you're a graduate—all grown up."

"I've also been all over the world—by myself in a lot of places. I think that qualifies me as an adult more than a piece of paper."

"I know. Just humor me, okay?" her mom said, wearing that mom-look that said, cut me some slack.

Arabella sighed with an exaggerated eye-roll. "Fine."

"So much attitude. I wonder who you could have gotten so much snark from," her mom wondered aloud even though we all knew.

Harry held up his hands. "Don't look at me."

We laughed, and more pictures were taken before we finally made our way to a local restaurant for dinner.

Harry loosened up a few drinks in, as predicted, and by the end of the night, we were all laughing, walking out to wait for our Uber.

"I don't know why you didn't just stay at our place," Arabella stated.

Her father looked between us and winced, but thankfully, Diana answered for him. "We prefer the hotel. Besides, we need our privacy," she murmured.

Arabella cringed. "Ew, Mom."

Their Uber pulled up, and her parents were still laughing when the door closed. Ours was right behind, and by the time we pulled up to the house, my hands were sweating and shaking.

Arabella had plans—big plans—and I was worried my surprise tonight would possibly put a kink in them.

God, what if she said no.

With a deep breath, I closed my eyes and opened the door.

She gasped, her hands shooting to her mouth as she took in the flickering candles and rose petals all over the foyer. She stepped over the threshold, and somehow my trembling legs followed her into the living room that mirrored the foyer décor.

"Willem," she breathed, spinning to take it all in.

Her eyes bounced between the candles and me, a mix of

excitement, love, and a hint of panic. I knew what she thought, and I just hoped she didn't kill me when she realized it wasn't that.

"I love your wild spirit," I started. "I love your adventure and freedom. I love that you have plans. I love that you took the future ahead of you and twisted them to fit your plans. I love you."

"I love you, too."

I closed the gap and held her hands in mine. "I know your hotels and tickets are booked, but I was hoping I could convince you to maybe shift for me."

She'd graduated with a bachelor's in marketing and international affairs. But long before graduation, she'd taken every study-abroad class she could and turned her love of travel into an online agency that planned trips for others. She also stumbled upon a love of writing, and travel blogs and magazines emailed her daily.

My girl had goals, and I hoped tonight didn't make her feel like I wanted to squash them. I just wanted to be part of them too.

But doubt crept it when her brows furrowed, and her hands tensed in mine. I slid my thumbs over the smooth skin, reassuring her.

Inhaling as far as I could, I stretched the band of nerves threatening to crush my lungs and looked her up and down. She was stunning with her dark, coppery hair illuminated by the flames, laying down her back, stark against the fitted white dress I'd done nothing but imagine pulling off. Standing there, an image of her in a much more formal white dress flashed, and one thought crossed my mind.

Someday. Someday, Arabella would be my wife.

But not today.

"I'm not teaching classes for the next few semesters. At least, not in-person classes. I signed up to take charge of the online portion classes and will be shaping that program over the next year."

"Uhhh...what?"

If anything, she looked more confused, and I leaned down to kiss the lines between her brows. "I also booked a one-way ticket to go with you on your travels...if you'll have me."

"What?" she practically screeched.

Her eyes stretched wide, and I held my breath, waiting for a reaction beyond shock. The point-two seconds of waiting could have been an eternity of standing on the edge of a cliff, unsure if I'd fall to the side with a net or free-fall into nothing.

"Are you fucking kidding me?" She did screech that time.

"Umm...no?"

Tears filled her eyes, and I imagined all the possibilities but one, pessimism at its best.

"Yes!" she finally shouted. "A thousand times, yes."

"Oh, thank fuck," I sighed, almost collapsing in relief.

"Did you really think I'd say no?"

"I just know how you like your independence, and we've only done short trips together. I honestly wasn't sure. College is over, and your life stretches like an open canvas ready for you to paint it. Anything can happen—anything can change."

"Willem..." She studied me and dropped my hands only to wrap them around my neck and burrow them in my hair to pull my mouth to hers. I relished in the reassurance her lips offered, fed from her confidence when mine somehow vanished. "I love you."

God, I'd never tire of hearing her say it. "I love you, too."

"If life is a canvas to be painted, then I want you to paint it with me. Who knows what it will turn out to be, but as long as you're with me, then it will be perfect."

"Yeah?"

"Hell, yes," she shouted.

Her mouth crashed to mine, only to jerk back so she could jump in excitement. If there was one thing I learned around

Arabella, it was to always be prepared, so I was ready when she jumped in my arms—but I still let her topple us to the couch.

Her dress rode up, and I drug my hands up her toned thighs, groaning at finally feeling her under my touch.

"Oh, thank god. I was so worried," she muttered between kisses.

"About what?"

"How the hell I was going to survive without your cock. I was going to put to the test if someone could die from sexual starvation."

I barked a laugh that quickly morphed to a moan when she bit her way down my neck. "We couldn't have that."

"No. In fact, I'm pretty hungry right now, Dr. Deander."

I drove my hand in her hair, fisting it tight to tug her back—taking control. "What are you hungry for?"

"You."

With a growl, I stood and laid her out on the floor, roughly shoving her dress up only to find her pussy bare.

"Yes," I hissed, ripping my pants open and wasting no time to bury myself between her thighs with a simple promise. "Just for a little while. I have to pack."

"Just for a little while," she agreed.

But we both knew it was a lie because it was a long while before we got up from that floor and even longer before we put any clothes on.

Exactly how I liked it.

Want more student-teacher romance? Check out the forbidden, best-selling romance, Voyeur.

Read for FREE with your Kindle Unlimited subscription.

Don't miss out on any of my upcoming books, giveaways, and important news by signing up for my newsletter... Fiona Cole Newsletter.
You can also join my Facebook reader group, Fiona Cole's Lovers, for exclusive sneak peeks and teasers.

Other Books by Fiona Cole

ALL BOOKS ARE FREE IN KINDLE UNLIMITED

The King's Bar Series
Where You Can Find Me
Deny Me
Imagine Me

Shame Me Not Series
Shame
Make It to the Altar (Shame Me Not 1.5)

The Voyeur Series
Voyeur
Lovers (Cards of Love)
Surrender (A Lovers Novella)
Savior
Another
Watch With Me (A Free Liar Prequel)
Liar
Teacher

Blame it on the Alcohol
Blame it on the Champagne
Blame it on the Tequila
Blame it on the Alcohol - Book 3 (Coming late 2021)

Standalones

Just for a Little While

About the Author

Fiona Cole is a military wife and a stay at home mom with degrees in biology and chemistry. As much as she loved science, she decided to postpone her career to stay at home with her two little girls, and immersed herself in the world of books until finally deciding to write her own.

Fiona loves hearing from her readers, so be sure to follow her on social media.

Email: authorfionacole@gmail.com
Newsletter
Reader Group: Fiona Cole's Lovers
www.authorfionacole.com

Made in the USA
Monee, IL
16 July 2025